TALES FROM
A WILD GOOSE'S
QUILL

RAY FLANAGAN

ASHRIDGE PRESS/COUNTRY BOOKS

Published by Ashridge Press
A subsidiary of Country Books
Courtyard Cottage, Little Longstone, Bakewell, Derbyshire DE45 1NN
Tel/Fax: 01629 640670
e-mail: dickrichardson@country-books.co.uk

ISBN 1 901214 77 X

British Library Cataloguing in Publication Data.
A catalogue record for this book is available from the British Library.

*In this work of fiction, the characters, places and events are
either the product of the author's imagination or they
are used entirely fictitiously.*

Appreciation

My gratitude to the publisher, Mr. Dick Richardson,
for his professionalism and trustworthiness

Printed and bound by:
CPI Antony Rowe Ltd

For Eva and Mohamed Khalifa
No nicer people

CONTENTS

Eros Creeps Into Roscommon

It was Brian's last year in primary school. There were nine boys and seven girls in his class. If Tommy O'Toole and Micky McMahon hadn't been kept back, for the second year running, there would have been seven boys and seven girls, all twelve-years-old. But O'Toole and McMahon, both fourteen, put up the average age, lowered the standard, and upset the gender balance. Besides, they were the only boys who wore long pants. Their voices, too, had broken.

From the first day on, O'Toole had his knife in Patrick O'Connor. O'Connor was a refined boy, tall and thin and serious, with a slight frown on his face. He was quietly-spoken, seldom laughed, never used bad language and wouldn't dream of peeing with the other boys against the back wall of the school when they got out to play: he used the lavatory. O'Toole, on the other hand, was squat, vulgar and very strong. He proudly pissed a steaming arc on the gable higher than anyone else's. One day in the yard O'Toole crept up behind O'Connor, caught him in his strong arms around the crotch, and lifted him wriggling from the ground. Brian saw the pain in Patrick O'Connor's face as he struggled free of O'Toole's clutches and straightened the belt again on his well-pressed short pants. When Patrick left primary school he went on to college and later became a missionary priest. He died of prostate cancer in Namibia at the age of thirty-three.

Brian kept out of Tommy O'Toole's way as much as he could. He hated his pimply face, and the tiny hairs

7

beginning to grow on his hard jaws. He hated his name, that rhymed with fool, and cruel, and mule. He would have loved to be able to fight him, but O'Toole was too strong for him and would have killed him in a fight. Once Brian's uncle from Dublin brought him a new football and when he took it to school next day, the first thing O'Toole said when they got out to play was, 'Here with your ball, O'Brien, or I'll break your fuckin' jaw!' Brian kicked it to him, but O'Toole missed it and Eamonn Maloney got it. He kicked it as high as he could up in the air and it landed in the branches of the yew tree. Brian was glad, because his ball was safe up there and O'Toole couldn't it.

Towards the beginning of that last year in primary school, the master was giving the class a dictation on 'The Wild Geese'. O'Toole and his friend, Micky McMahon, were sat on their own in the back seat. Once again O'Toole, who never did any homework, was copying from McMahon, who never did any homework either. Brian was sitting in the row in front of them, between Maeve Mulrennan, who had wiry blonde hair, and Josephine Finan, who had brown wavy hair. When they had finished the dictation, the master went down and picked up Tommy O'Toole's jotter to have a look.

'Good Christ,' he said, getting red in the face as he walked back to the front of the class, 'another masterpiece from O'Toole!'

The teacher was a Cork man whose passions were easily aroused. He stood tall and erect, and he brooked no nonsense. The veins now bulged out on his pink head as he stamped over to the easel, rammed the two pegs into their holes, plonked the blackboard on them and, looking at O'Toole's jotter, wrote on the board with a new stick of white chalk: *Patrick Sarsfield never felt attle the ship began to sale*. For a moment the class was unsure how to react, but when the master drew a big, violent circle around *attle* and *sale* (the chalk breaking in two), they all roared with dutiful laughter at the stupidity of it. But Brian glanced sideways into Maeve Mulrennan's jotter and saw that she had written *attel* and *sail*. Josephine Finan, on his other side, had *attil* and *sale*. Brian, one of the best in the class, had, of course, written *until* and *sail*, though he wasn't too sure what the master had said because of his south-of-Ireland accent. Anyway, Maeve Mulrennan and Josephine Finan shouldn't have laughed, the ignoramuses. Brian overheard O'Toole's whispered threat to Micky McMahon in the seat behind him: 'If you ever gimme the wrong spellin' again, I'll put my boot up your arse!' But it wasn't McMahon's fault if O'Toole had copied from him.

It was better keep away from Tommy O'Toole.

Micky McMahon, O'Toole's best friend, wasn't much better. He was a tough codger, too, a real ruffian with a filthy tongue and two green eyes like a goat. He was always drawing pictures in his copybook of big girls with lots of hair. 'Nice little hoors,' Brian heard him say once to O'Toole. He didn't know the word, but it sounded dark and sinister. Maeve Mulrennan hated McMahon because he said her wiry blonde hair was like a straw rope around a scarecrow, and Josephine Finan hated the two of them because one day they looked in under the lavatory door when she was on the toilet and ever since they would snigger and pull faces and make jokes about her whenever she was near.

Nobody would sit in the back seat with Tommy O'Toole and Micky McMahon.

One Sunday evening, shortly after Christmas, Brian O'Brien begged his mammy to give him the money to go to the pictures in Tobbercastle. There was a Laurel and Hardy film on that night.

'We're still on holidays, mammy, so I don't have to be up for school in the morning.'

9

'There's heavy clouds in the sky and the wind is rising,' said his mother. 'I think you'd better wait till some other time.'

'But this is the last night the Laurel and Hardy film is on.'

His mother reluctantly gave way.

'Okay, then,' she said, 'but don't forget to take your raincoat with you. And make sure the light on your bike is working. It will be dark on your way home.'

Brian got excited. The long seven miles into Tobbercastle didn't daunt him in the least. A lot of it was downhill and the wind would be on his back going into town. He gobbled down the thick piece of buttered bread with the scallions that his mother insisted he should eat before he left, slipped into his new fawn coat that was much too long for him, jumped on his bicycle and hit off as fast as he could down the road to Tobbercastle and Laurel and Hardy. The raincoat, of course, he forgot, and the dynamo was out of order.

It was pitch dark when Brian came out of the cinema. The wind was now blowing fiercely, and the rain was lashing down. Then Teddy Melvin, the cattle jobber, saw Brian as he was about to get up on his bicycle.

'Listen, O'Brien,' he said, 'I'll give you a lift home in the back of the truck. But you'll have to cycle out to the end of the town first. I'll pick you up around Bligh's corner when the coast is clear. The guards here in Tobbercastle are right hoors on us country lads.' That word again!

It was decent enough of Melvin, for he wasn't supposed to carry passengers in his cattle truck. And he didn't have a tax disc either!

Brian set off down the town in the rain. Only then did he realize his dynamo wasn't working. Trembling in case those guards with that appalling name would pull him for not having a light on his bicycle and he from the country, he took a short cut up an alleyway, around by the back of the swimming-pool and down through the wood. He arrived out on the main road again a little beyond Bligh's corner. He hoped he hadn't missed Melvin. The wind and the rain were in his face now. Seven miles was a long way home. Where was Melvin? Then, to his immense relief, he heard the rattling truck coming along the road. Melvin pulled up beside him and he climbed up over the side crate into the back, lifting his bicycle in after him. They started out, but hardly had they gone fifty metres when the truck swerved suddenly in to the side of the road again and shuddered to a halt in a spasm of jerks. Thrown completely off balance, Brian tripped over the bar of his bike and fell into a soft, wet cowpat.

'God blast it!' he said, smelling the dung in the dark and knowing that his fawn topcoat of pure new wool was now in a mess. 'There'll be trouble tomorrow when my mother sees this?'

That piece of swearing was the nearest Brian had yet come to using a bad word. Wondering why Melvin had stopped and at the same time trying to wipe the dirt off with his white linen handkerchief, he suddenly saw through the side-crate of the truck two shadowy figures silhouetted against a barren tree at the side of the road. His heart gave a great thud when he saw who it was: Tommy O'Toole and Micky McMahon. Micky was sat astride the hard, firm bar of his bicycle, his long legs touching the ground on either side, a hump on him like a cat in the rain. Tommy O'Toole was pumping wind like mad into the back tyre of his all-steel Raleigh. Micky had wellingtons on and a rain cape, and Tommy was wearing LDF boots with thongs for laces, and a green frieze topcoat. The heads of both were bare in the rain, and they had no lights on their bicycles either.

Melvin turned down the window as far as it would go

and shouted,

'What's up, lads?'

'Cow down,' O'Toole shouted back. 'Is that you Melvin, you bastard? Switch off your bloody headlamps.'

'I thought you liked headlamps,' said Melvin, with a dirty laugh.

'He does,' said Mahon with a snigger, 'and so do I!'

'Were ye at the pics?' Melvin asked, 'I didn't see ye there.'

Two volcanic guffaws erupted simultaneously from the throats of McMahon and O'Toole. The rumblings developed into deep, sleazy belly-laughs with giggles rattling in them, pride-filled grunts, evil chesty brays with a touch of shame in them. They were sounds Brian had never heard before from anyone. The two of them came out from under the tree and wheeled their bicycles over to the side of Melvin's throbbing truck. Brian cowered low in the back, hoping desperately that they wouldn't spot him, or that Melvin wouldn't give them a lift, too.

'No, we weren't at the pics!'

'And where have ye been on a night like this?' asked Melvin.

'You tell him,' said McMahon to O'Toole, throwing his legs over the bar again.

O'Toole sat on the carrier of his own bike and put his right foot up on the running-board of the truck. He seemed to enjoy the vibrations of the engine running up his leg.

'Well, if you want to know …,' he said.

McMahon gave him a great thump in the ribs and again they broke out into that dark, hideous, uncontrollable laugh.

'Out with it, for Jasus' sake,' said Melvin, sensing there was something great coming.

O'Toole said: 'Alright, Teddy. We're after ridin' two women over there in the San!'

'What!' said Teddy, 'On a night like this! And at your age!'

Melvin was in no way inclined to believe their story.

'And who were the two birds?'

'Haven't a clue. Didn't get their names,' said O'Toole.

'I did,' said McMahon, 'Biddy Blackbird and Tessie Thrush! Ha! Ha! ha!'

Just then, on full beam, the lights of a squad car came round the corner. Melvin switched off the engine. Micky and Tommy scurried off as fast as they could in among the trees. 'Keep your bollocksy head down,' Melvin whispered to Brian in the back. Crouching as low as he could, Brian watched the squad car as it began to slow down. It came creeping up alongside the truck, drove slowly by, then gathered speed again, and was gone. After a short wait, Melvin switched on his lights, pulled the choke, shouted 'Well done, lads!' to the two fugitives, and moved off into the wet night in a cloud of smoke and fumes. Brian could hear O'Toole cursing and blinding and calling out to Melvin to give them a lift home. The wind had gone out of his back tyre again.

The words he had heard from O'Toole burnt deep into Brian's mind. That night he decided he would make use of the silly diary with the white cover and pink flowers that his sister Kay had given him as a Christmas present. His first entry was, ATWARTWOTITS. He thought it wiser just to write the first letters down, in case he ever lost the diary or somebody read it. He put a heavy ring around the R.

*   *   *

Of the seven girls in the class, Rose Kenny with the ginger hair and the freckles on her nose was the one Brian now liked best. She was very good-natured. In her lunch sand-

13

wiches she always had a thick layer of sugar spread over the home-made butter. Too much sugar was bad for you, his mammy used to say, and that was why some children had runny noses all the time. Rose had a runny nose, too, but Brian didn't mind that because one night, shortly after the Easter holidays, a varicose vein in his mammy's right leg burst, and the blood and pus spread all over the clean sheets, and she couldn't get up the next morning to make him his lunch, and Brian had nothing to eat in school, so Rose gave him a bite of her sandwich, the middle bit where it was very soft and sweet and juicy, and he never forgot that.

When May came, the month of the Blessed Virgin, his mammy was alright again. Mrs. Heffernan, the master's wife, took them for singing. They were practising *Bring flowers of the rarest* for the May devotions in the church and everybody was supposed to bring a bunch of flowers to school on the first Friday in May because that was the day the P.P. was coming to hear them sing.

'Now don't forget the flowers tomorrow,' said Mrs. Heffernan on the Thursday. And you must all come in your best clothes, with your fingernails clean and your shoes shining. I don't want anybody looking like a tinker when the priest comes. And another thing: Fr. Smallhorn is very fond of poetry and he might ask one or two of you to recite a poem. So be prepared, all of you!"

When they got out to play, O'Toole and McMahon came over to Brian.

'O'Brien,' said O'Toole, 'you're supposed to be very smart. If Smallhorn asks anyone to recite a poem tomorrow, as sure as shit it'll be you. Have you one ready?'

'Not yet,' said Brian, 'but I was thinking…'

'Look,' said O'Toole, 'I have a good poem for you. The P.P. will love it. Have you anywhere to write it down?'

Without thinking, Brian produced his little white diary.

'Jasus, will ye look at this,' said O'Toole to McMahon. 'An' all them daft flowers on the cover!'

'What's in it?' asked McMahon.

O'Toole thumbed through the white diary with his dirty, sweaty fingers. There was only the one entry.

'What in Christ's name does that word mean?' said O'Toole, when he saw ATWARTWOTITS. Brian tightened his lips and wouldn't answer. How glad he was now that he had not written the words out in full. The bell rang for the end of play.

'Quick, let me write the poem down for you. And if Smallhorn calls on you to recite tomorrow, you'd better say this poem or you might never get the chance to say a second one!'

Then in big letters he printed 6 lines inside the back cover of the diary, closed it and handed it back to Brian. There was no time to read them.

Brian didn't like flowers. Girls were always making silly necklaces with them or sticking them in their hair. On his way to school the next morning, Brian didn't take the main road through the village but went through the wood, looking for flowers for Mrs. Heffernan. He wasn't supposed to go through the wood. His daddy had told him often enough to stick to the main road. Connolly's bull used to graze on the patches of sweet grass among the old, twisted trees. At the edge of the wood where the land sloped away towards the lake it was wet and swampy, and down there somewhere was the swally-hole, that had no bottom. The muddy water that seeped through the sluice at the end of the lake got sucked down there, and if you went too near it you might sink in the swamp and never be able to get out. At the other end of the wood there was the old round tower that once rose up proud and sturdy and solid, but now tilted limp and lifeless among the bracken and brushwood that luxuriated around its base, only the tough

15

arms of the ivy that embraced it keeping it from collapsing altogether. Two round rocks had fallen from the top of the tower and lay half buried in the ground beside it. You never knew when the whole thing might come tumbling down on top of you.

Brian's father did not want him going through the wood.

There was a wishing-well in the wood, too, a tiny spring of fresh water that came gurgling out among a circle of mossy stones. Long ago St. Patrick had stopped there for a drink on his way to spend forty days praying and fasting on the top of Croagh Patrick. First Brian found some primroses on a sunny bank running along inside the low stone wall at the edge of the wood. But it took a lot of picking to get a good fistful of primroses. He shifted on till he came to the damper ground near the wishing-well and the marshy lakeland. There he came on a lot of sturdy, deep-yellow buttercups and he soon had his hands full of their big, swollen, sappy stems. It was then he noticed the shadow slowly creeping up on him. He looked up quickly. There was Connolly's bull, only two metres away. His heart began to race, his temples pounded. He wished now he had obeyed his father and kept to the main road. He wished he had stuck to the primroses. Most of all, he wished he was out of the wood and safe in school. The bull looked at him, then lowered his head, and continued grazing peacefully around the well. Brian stole gingerly away, dodged quickly among the trees and never stopped running till he reached the round tower. There he had to pause for a quick pee, looking over his shoulder to see if the bull was following him. Then he continued running till he reached the school. He had lost half his flowers.

He was last into class. With embarrassment he deposited his primroses and buttercups on the teacher's table and took his place among his classmates, who were stood in a semi-circle around the room, singing. Then he heard Maureen Gilligan giggling. Mary Fitz began to giggle, too. Tommy O'Toole grunted and smirked. Patrick O'Connor seemed to be deliberately looking the other way, a deeper frown than usual on his forehead. What was going on? Brian glanced at Rose Kenny. She was very red in the face, but her eyes were glued to her songbook. Then Micky McMahon, who was standing beside him, gave Brian a dig in the ribs and whispered awful loud, 'Close your duck-house, your drake is coming out!' Convulsions of laughter went round the class. Brian looked down. Sure enough, his fly was wide open. In the hurry he had forgotten to close it. The blood rushed to his head. He knew he was scarlet. He glanced over again at Rose Kenny. Had she laughed with the others? He didn't know what to do. He couldn't go buttoning up in front of the whole class. There were five buttonholes in the new pants his mother had made for him and they were still a bit too small for the big grey buttons and he knew he couldn't close them quickly. If only he had a zip like Johnny Judge, the tailor's son.

Then the teacher said, 'These flowers of yours, Brian, need a lot of water. Go out to the pump and bring me in a bucketful.'

Brian skipped out as fast as he could. He had plenty of time now to solve his problem. When he came back they were just finishing the chorus:

Oh Mary, we crown thee with blossoms today,
Queen of the angels and queen of the May.

'You were a long time with the water,' Mrs. Heffernan said. 'What kept you? Your buttercups are withering already.'

'He had to close …' Mary Fitz started, but the rest was so funny, she just couldn't get it out. She shook and shook.

'What are you laughing at, you faggot,' said the teacher. 'If you don't stop this minute, you'll get the rod.'

Mary subsided, but Brian noticed she still seemed to be

shaking a bit under her pink cotton blouse. Mary was a big girl for her age.

'Now don't forget to stand up when Fr. Smallhorn comes,' said the teacher, 'and when we're singing *Bring flowers of the rarest* I don't want the crows to join in. Do you hear, Josephine Finan and Maureen Gilligan? And if he asks anyone to say a poem, I want you to stand up and come out here to the front and recite it loud and clear. I hope you all have a poem off by heart, like I told you!'

Brian froze where he was standing. He had forgotten about the poem. He had left his diary at home. O'Toole's eyes were piercing him from across the room. Then the doorbell rang and in came the postman. He waved to all the children before handing Mrs. Heffernan a note. When he left, the teacher read the note and then announced to the class:

'Fr. Smallhorn has just sent me word that he cannot, unfortunately, come today. He's having trouble with his bicycle again. The wind has gone out of his back tyre. He'll be coming on Monday.'

O'Toole looked at McMahon and gave a forced cough. Brian thanked God secretly for the P.P.'s puncture.

When they were going home from school that Friday afternoon, Rose said to Brian:

'Your flowers were lovely. Where did you get them?'

'Over the wood,' said Brian.

'Will you show me where?'

'It's too dangerous. Connolly's bull is there.'

What was the real reason, Brian wondered, why all girls liked flowers so much? Was it the colours, or the petals, or the smell or the shape? Did they feel like flowers themselves? He laughed at the idea of the seven girls in his class stuck in a vase on Mrs. Heffernan's desk with water up to their necks. His mother grew pansies and marigolds in the front garden, near the two lilac bushes that had such a strong scent in May. She used to cut the lilac blossoms and put them in water in a little glass bottle that served as a vase beneath the Blessed Virgin's statue in the kitchen. Now and again the top-heavy lilacs would cause the bottle-vase to topple over and spill onto the settle-bed where he used to sleep with his sister till he went away to college. The bed would be wet in the morning. Maybe that was why he did not like flowers.

The following Monday, however, as he was leaving for school, Brian took a marigold from the bed of flowers in the front garden, when his mother wasn't watching. He slipped it into Rose Kenny's hand in the school yard, when the others weren't watching. Rose loved it, although marigolds don't smell nice, especially in spring when they're full of sap. But that morning Rose had a very runny nose again, so she couldn't smell them anyway.

Brian liked going to school, most days. He and Sheila O'Nolan were the best in the class. Sheila was the best at sums, he was the best at Irish and English. They were both very good at recitation. Sheila generally had the edge on him in bible history. But it was the geography lessons that Brian loved most of all, especially when Mrs. Heffernan would branch off from the principal towns of each county, and the capital cities and main rivers of every country in Europe, and start talking about the trees and the birds and the animals and the insects. He would sit in front of her, eyes wide open, listening to every detail and full of admiration for all the things she knew.

Brian's biggest problem was blotting. Though he had a way with words and made up very nice sentences, he could never write a composition and keep his page clean. If Mrs. Heffernan was in bad humour, she would give him a smart smack of the wooden ruler across his thin fingers for every big, blue blot. One cold morning in April she gave him five slaps on the same hand with her cane because he had two blots that went right through to the next page as well.

'You slovenly little imp,' she said, 'Have you never heard of blotting-paper? I'm surprised your mother allowed you to bring such a filthy jotter to school.'

The pain of the slaps made Brian's eyes fill with tears. Besides, he had no lunch in his schoolbag. Mrs. Heffernan was in very bad twist that morning. Her husband, the doctor, had to go out on an emergency call the evening before and hadn't come back yet, so he couldn't drive her to school, which was a mile away from the dispensary, and she had to foot it all the way, though the road was a bit slippery from overnight frost, and she was a heavy woman and did not like walking. When she was giving Brian the blotting slaps she couldn't have known, of course, that his mammy's varicose vein had burst the night before and her husband was doing his best at that very moment to get it to clot. If he didn't, she might bleed to death. That was the day Rose Kenny gave him the best part of her sandwich.

Brian was a little bit afraid of Sheila O'Nolan, the brainy girl, his only real rival in the class. For one thing, she was a bit of a tell-tale. You had to be careful what you said to her. Like himself, she had black, curly hair and brown eyes. Some whispered suspiciously that she looked more like Brian than his sister Kay did, with her blonde hair and blue eyes. But if Brian was a bit afraid of Sheila, it was her daddy that really gave him the willies. He was a tall, strong man with a deep voice, a funny accent and a stiff leg. At Mass on Sundays he used to sit in the back row on the men's side, his big, rigid leg stretched proudly out into the aisle. On his way up to the front, Brian was always terrified in case he'd come to grief over the leg. Mr. O'Nolan had a set pedal on his bicycle so that when he pushed with his right leg the left one did not move. To throw his leg over the bar, he had to pull the bicycle in under himself and then straighten up. Getting off, it was the other way round. Brian sometimes had nightmares about that leg.

One evening, about an hour after Brian had got home from school, Mr. O'Nolan dismounted awkwardly from his bicycle right outside their house and rang his bell loud and long. Brian looked through the curtains of the front window and when he saw who it was, he knew what was up and he began to shiver. Sheila had told. Just what he was afraid of. He hadn't meant any harm. In fact he didn't know he had said anything bad at all. He was only trying to be funny. It was like this. Sheila loved horses, and every day after school she would gallop all the long way home, her head to the side, whinnying from time to time, changing into a trot when she was winded, pawing at the ground and only stopping to eat the fresh green grass outside the fairgreen wall. That day after school Brian and his friend, Eamonn Maloney – great footballers of the future – were kicking a battered tin can along the road and smudging their good shoes – more trouble when Brian got home – and shouting 'Up Roscommon!' with every kick, when Sheila came trotting by.

'Wouldn't you like to have a jockey to ride you?' Brian shouted after her. The mare came to a dead halt. Eamonn nearly split his sides laughing at what Brian had said.

'I'll tell when I get home, so I will,' said Sheila the mare. 'You're a rotten, filthy-minded dog, so you are, Brian O'Brien!' For the life of him Brian couldn't see anything wrong with a jockey riding a horse, but there was something about the way his friend laughed that made him feel uneasy. Eamonn took a flying kick at the can and lofted it high in the air in over the hedge.

'And it's over the bar. The winning point for Roscommon!' he said, with glee.

And there was the leg now, ringing the bell of his bike for all he was worth. Brian's mother went out to him.

'What's up, Peter,' she said.

'Up!' said Mr. O'Nolan, 'Up! There's a lot up. Nobody should know better than yourself, sweetie, when there's something up! Now you go in, Molly O'Brien, and tell that skittery-arsed corrabuckeen of yours that if he ever says dirty things to our Sheila again, I'll come right down from the house and make his little pizzle sizzle!'

With that he swung the leg over the crossbar and rode off home, puffing hard as he pedalled up the hill.

After that Brian was very careful what he said to Sheila O'Nolan at school. Or to Tommy O'Toole. In fact, he gradually became very careful of what he said to anyone at all. It was so easy to be misunderstood. He began to talk less and less, that last year in school. He just listened carefully to what everybody else was saying but kept quiet himself.

'Brian has grown very silent of late,' the teacher told his mother one day after Mass. 'He seems to be withdrawing into himself a bit. I wonder why.'

When his mother raised the subject with Brian, he just shrugged his shoulders and made no reply. How could he explain? She wouldn't really understand. After all, it was she herself who was very fond of saying, 'The less said the easiest mended.' Mrs. O'Brien decided she'd have a little talk with Fr. Smallhorn when he came round to make his annual call.

*   *   *

Though Brian liked going to school, he always looked forward to the holidays – not so much the Christmas holidays, because the weather was always cold and wet then, and there wasn't much to do outside. There were no leaves on the trees, the fields were dull and water-logged, the flowers were dead, and the few robins and blackbirds in the garden were silent and droopy and seemed to have no life left in their limp little bodies. But when spring came round everything began to fill up again with colours and sounds and activity and at the beginning of the Easter holidays his father would always say, 'Now, me son, there's work to be done,' and that meant only one thing: a week in the bog cutting the turf. Brian just loved the bog.

It was the same that last year in school. Easter Monday, up early, into the wellingtons and old working clothes, out with the bicycles and off to the bog. Brian was so happy to be alone with his father, to be able to help him with the hard work of cutting the turf, to share with him the lovely loneliness of the bog, without either of them saying a word. His father tied the loy and the slane firmly to the crossbar of his bike with two pieces of rope. The slane had a very sharp blade and Brian noticed that his father threw his leg very slowly and carefully over the bar when getting up on his bike. A bit like Mr. O'Nolan.

'I'll send Kay down with the lunch in a couple of hours,' said Mrs. O'Brien as they waved good-bye and headed off for the bog. 'Plenty of crispy fried eggs in the sand-wiches,' Brian called back, as they were disappearing round the corner. There was no point in asking his mammy to put sugar in them.

They left their bikes inside the hedge when they arrived at the bog. There was still fresh dew and wisps of gossamer on the grass and heather as they crossed the 300 metres over to the bank of turf where the cutting stopped the year before and the wheelbarrow still lay upside down across a tussock of sedge, its two shafts like legs spread-eagled in the air. The bank had to be cleaned first of the tough, rooty heather before the cutting proper could begin. Brian sat on a dry spongy patch of ground where the sun was shining and watched his able-bodied father clean the bank with his sturdy loy. He threw the scraws down into the hollow: they would provide a firm footing for Brian later when he was catching the sods of turf and putting them on the barrow. While waiting for his father to finish cleaning the bank, Brian stretched out full length on his back. The bog was his Garden of Eden. In the bog he felt free. He looked up into the sunny blue sky. He listened to the light breeze singing through the sedges, he felt it again tingle along his skin. Once more he let his thoughts wander off through the endless freedom of the turbary. That lovely word he had learned from Mrs. Heffernan. Other lovely bog words came into his mind: the ceannabhan, the spadach, the salleys, the bulrushes, the bog-butter, the lady-ferns. Brian's mind rested on these words, he pillowed his head on them, he let them dance around in his memory. But now, for the first time, other words, strange and ugly, intruded on his paradise. He couldn't keep them out. They were the words Tommy O'Toole and Micky McMahon used at school. They were the words Melvin used. They were the threatening words and strange language Mr. O'Nolan used with his mother. They were the unguarded words he said himself to Sheila that caused the trouble in the first place with Mr. O'Nolan. There was his own coded word in his diary, with the ring around the R.

Brian began to feel uneasy and restless. He turned on his side and looked at the bank of turf his father was working on. He had never noticed before the way the colours on the side of the turf-bank changed from the top to the bottom. On the upper level was the spadach, the tough undergrowth that his father was now laboriously removing with the loy in order to get to the good, soft turf lower down. Later he would cut through this with his slane, its right-angled blades carving with pleasure the shapely sods that warmed the hearth and the heart in winter. The top was light-coloured, blonde, fair, then changed imperceptibly into a light brown, brunette, and became darker lower down until

24

it became a juicy, shiny black, the best turf of all. 'Old trees and vegetable matter,' Mrs. Heffernan explained in school, 'that rotted away thousands of years ago. That's what bogs are made of.' Brian couldn't imagine the bog once full of vegetables. There were bog beans, alright, but then they were only flowers that grew, like the marsh marigolds, down by the stream near the pliant salleys. On the other hand, if there were carrots and parsnips all over the bog once, that would explain the ginger-blonde-brown of the top layers of peat, the same colour as Rose Kenny's hair. That made him think of sweet sugar sandwiches, and he began to feel a little pang of hunger already, though it couldn't have been much more than 10 o'clock. The bog air made you feel wicked hungry after a very short while.

Brian's restlessness increased. He turned over on his stomach and lay tense along the receptive, spongy moss-bank beneath him, his face now in the other direction, away from his father. About him were little hillocks of heather, patches of gorse and dense bracken, runs of pink marshmallows, stretches of brown-tipped flaggers, clumps of the carnivorous Venus flytrap with the sensitive hairs that meant certain death for the unwary insect that crossed them. In front of his eyes a host of pismires were struggling with an infinitesimal clod of last year's turf, erecting some barrier or monument along the maze of routes criss-crossing the vast, unending reaches of the bog's surface. Two powerful earwigs in tandem passed them by, unmindful of the problems of their fellow species, unhelpful, more important matters on their minds. Brian focused his eyes further afield. All about the bog the ceannabhan was in bloom, the white heads bobbing about in the breeze on supple stems. Bog cotton, Mrs. Heffernan said, was the English name. Were those white balls of any use, he wondered. In his geography book there was a picture of black men picking cotton in Alabama. There

25

they made cloth out of the cotton balls.

Brian's eyes narrowed as his vision focussed further away, out over their own bog and all the neighbouring bogs, out across the parish boundary, way beyond the county border altogether, back to the very end of the great western plain where he could see the twin mountain peaks of Nephin Beg and Nephin Mor a great distance away. There they were on that lovely April day, jutting up firm and pointed against the hazy horizon. Most days they were invisible, modestly draped in mists or fogs or clouds rolling in off the Atlantic. Today they were exposed. Where exactly were those peaks, he asked himself. He knew they were near Croagh Patrick, The Reek, a long way off on the coast of Mayo. On the other side of the ocean was America. Why was the mountain called The Reek? Were there reeks of turf up there, too? One day he would find out for himself. One day he would go and see. One day he would mount those peaks. And he would go to America, to Alabama, to the cotton fields. Was that where cotton blouses were made? Suddenly Mary Fitz appeared in his mind, laughing.

Still strangely restive, Brian rolled over on his back again. He turned his head eastwards to see how far his father had got. He had almost finished cleaning the bank. Soon the turf-cutting proper would begin. Suddenly a small swarm of working honey bees landed near him on a tuft of blossoming, purple heather. 'Hurlers' his father used to call them, because of their black and yellow stripes that reminded him of the Kilkenny team. Once Brian had asked Rose Kenny if she played hurling – he thought that was very funny because of her name – but Rose just said he was daft. Now a queen bee appeared in the air, accompanied by six or seven drones. The queen was the one with the long, slender body whereas the sturdy drones had strong, hairy hind legs and thick abdomens. Brian knew all this from Mrs. Heffernan. There was great buzzing and zig-zagging going on over his head. After a flurry of excitement one of the drones seemed to get tired: he dropped to the ground and got lost in a cluster of ferns near where Brian was lying. 'The Latin name for the honey bee – Latin, as you know, is the queen of all languages – is 'apis mellifera',' Mrs. Heffernan explained. 'The nuptial flight of the queen bee takes place each year towards the end of April or the beginning of May, when she is about 8-days-old. On the flight she is accompanied by six to eight drones.' Was that the nuptial flight now? Brian had wanted to ask the teacher what exactly the nuptial flight was, but Micky Mahon and Tommy O'Toole were sniggering and tittering in the back seat and Brian was afraid to say anything. It might be the wrong thing again. Then he spotted the fallen drone just as the lobes of a Venus flytrap leaf snapped shut and devoured him. The swarm of worker bees rose up all at once from the heather and moved off over the bog. When he looked up, Brian saw that the queen and the other drones had moved on, too. High above in the clear sky a lark was trilling. He could just make out the little white feathers in her tail and the erectile crest on her head. He listened as she sang her chest out. When she stopped, she came swooping down to her nest on the ground, deliberately landing some distance away from it. The last few metres she would walk home in a crouched position, unnoticed, giving nothing away. The cleverness of it!

Then he heard another bird call. That was what he was hoping for, that was the sound that he could never forget, that was the first thing that came into his mind, that stirred in his memory, any time the bog was mentioned, that was what he longed to hear, but did not always hear, every time he was in the bog. It was the long, liquid, circling, diminishing warble of the curlew. Funnily enough, he had never actually seen a curlew, but he was somehow glad that he hadn't. He knew that even if she was the most beautiful bird in the world, her appearance could never match that wonderful, haunting refrain that cast a spell over the bog by day, like the will-o'-the-wisp did at night. He listened to the last notes of her tune curl and fade away and then, to his surprise, there followed a shrill, piercing whistle. It took him a few seconds to realise that it was his father beckoning him to come over with the wheelbarrow to the bank of turf. The cutting was about to begin.

Brian took off his jacket. His shirt was torn at the collar, his pullover was beginning to rip at the elbows, and there was a big hole in the seat of his old jeans, so that his underpants showed through. But they were working clothes, and nobody would see him in the bog anyway, so it didn't matter. To keep his long, black curls out of his eyes, he wore a soiled tweed cap belonging to his father, two sizes too big, with the peak to the back. Now for some hard work.

Brian caught the soft, wet sods of blonde turf in his arms as his father slewed them off the slane from the upper part of the bank. He placed them nicely in rows on the barrow and when he had about twenty on – there was room for a lot more, but twenty was enough because they were so heavy – he wheeled them out some thirty metres on the level ground, tipped the barrow sideways, and returned for the next haul. While Brian was wheeling out and back, his father could relax a bit, but with each emptied barrowful the distance back to the bank was getting shorter and shorter and the open area was gradually filling up with little heaps of peat sods that would later have to be scattered by hand so that the wind could dry them. Every so often Brian would glance up towards the hedge where they had left their bicycles, hoping his sister would soon appear at the gap with the lunch. After an hour on the wheelbarrow he was ravenous.

They worked on through the morning. His father was on the second spit now and the colour of the turf was changing to brunette. If the weather held, he would be half way down the bank by the end of the day. Then they heard the peal of the church bell from far away. They bared their heads, cast their eyes to the ground, and said the Angelus together aloud. As Brian was putting his cap back on he caught a glimpse of what he was most longing to see at that moment. His sister had just entered the bog from the road and was coming towards them, carrying the lunch basket on her arm. But to his astonishment, he saw that she was not alone: there was another girl with her. In the distance he couldn't make out who she was. Unaccountably, the question that Melvin asked O'Toole and McMahon that night after the pictures now came into his mind: 'And who were the two birds?' Feeling in high spirits because lunch was now so near, and feeling even more at ease with his father after they had prayed together, Brian thought it might be fun to ask a similar question of his father, though he had lately learned to be very careful about what he said to anyone. He decided to chance it.

'Here's Kay with the lunch,' he said, 'but she's not on her own. Who's the other bird with her?'

His father leant on the slane and looked him in the eyes. He could find no words for a few moments. He was completely taken by surprise by his son's question. When he recovered his speech, he said:

'Now what kind of a way is that to go talking about girls! Who taught you that kind of corner-boy language? I've never heard you come out with that sort of thing before. I'm afraid you're getting a bit too big for your boots, me bucko!'

Brian was never so embarrassed in his life. 'That's the end,' he said to himself, 'never again! I'll go off and join the Cistercians when I leave school. They are only allowed to talk on Christmas Day!'

By now the two lunch-bringers were fairly near. Then Brian recognised the girl who was helping Kay carry the lunch. It was – of all people in the world – Rose Kenny! She had a shopping-bag in her hand with two flasks of tea in it. Already embarrassed by his father, Brian was utterly mortified by the appearance of Rose Kenny. What was she doing here? She had no right to come intruding into his bog. His sister Kay was just as bad, bringing her along and exposing him like this in his torn pullover and filthy jeans, and his hands and arms covered in bog dirt. Girls had no feelings, they understood nothing.

Kay and Rose came closer, chatting and giggling all the way. Were they laughing at him? Was Rose making fun of him? He was so ashamed. What should he do or say? He made up his mind: he wouldn't say one word to either of them, not even 'Hello'. He would ignore them, and he would ignore his father, too. When they came up, the two girls greeted cheerily as they placed the basked and the shopping bag on the ground. Brian took a quick look at Rose, at what she was wearing, and then turned away. He couldn't believe his eyes. Was this some kind of a joke? She had on a magnificent, yellow dress, with black stripes – the Kilkenny colours. The colours of the bees. He had never seen that dress on her before. Was she, too, on a nuptial flight here in the bog? Was she looking for a drone? Betrayed by his sister, feeling so small and impure in the presence of immaculate Rose Kenny, Brian decided he would not drink the tea or touch the sandwiches. He was deeply hurt and had lost his appetite. He went over and lay once more on the mossy mound, face downwards again. He closed his eyes.

In silence, Brian's father started on the crisp, fried-egg sandwiches and the tea, ignoring his son. The girls went off to pick marsh marigolds and bog beans down among the salleys at the edge of the watercourse. When his father had finished, he lit a cigarette and sat smoking it on the wheel of the barrow. He had left three sandwiches in the basket. Brian was now on the verge of tears. His feelings were all in turmoil. Everything had changed, there were dark clouds hanging over his Garden of Eden. Kay and Rose returned, their fists full of bright, fresh flowers. They picked up the basket and shopping-bag and came over to where Brian was lying, to say good-bye. He lay there motionless. He could feel the ground vibrating under their feet. Out of the side of his eye he saw Rose's shapely ankle only inches away from him. He desperately wanted them to disappear, to go very far away, to depart from the bog quickly and leave him alone. 'Leave him,' said Kay, 'I think he's asleep.' Then as Rose's ankle turned away, a single yellow marigold landed on the ground beside Brian's head. The girls left the bog again as they had come, giggling and chatting, and now nibbling at the three tasty sandwiches that were left over.

Soon his father's whistle called Brian back to work. He rose slowly. His step was heavy now as he wheeled the barrow in and out. The clouds that were never absent too long from the sky over the bog grew darker. It became more and more overcast as the afternoon wore on. A light mist began to fall and it got noticeably cooler. The sods got heavier and heavier, and Brian's tired arms began to drop them more often. No more bees came by that afternoon, nor did the curlew call. Somehow there was a blight on the bog now. There would be no will-o'-the-wisp out that night to dance flings with the ghosts over the heath.

Though he was starving when he got home in the evening, the first thing that Brian did was have a good shower. He threw his filthy shirt and jeans into the laundry basket, shampooed his hair and scrubbed every trace of bog dirt from around his ears and under his fingernails. The water was black as it flowed off his tired body. He dressed in fresh, clean clothes, sprayed some of his sister's eau de toilette about his neck and ears and went into the kitchen, where his mother had a bowl of steaming vegetable soup waiting for him on the table. His father had already eaten and gone out to feed the calves. Kay had gone to the pictures in Tobbercastle..

Brian went to bed early, but before he switched off the light he took out his diary and wrote in it TWOBIRDS. It was only his second entry.

* * *

By the end of the Easter holidays the turf was cut and spread. Back at school Brian had to work hard for his Primary Cert. He kept himself to himself more than ever now. He avoided Tommy O'Toole and Micky McMahon like the plague. Whenever he was talking to Sheila O'Nolan he was careful to stick to the topics of sums or Irish or arithmetic. He never discussed with her what Mrs. Heffernan used to tell them about nature and wild life. He hardly ever looked Rose Kenny or Mary Fitz in the eye. Eamonn Maloney remained his best friend. They walked home from school together most days, sometimes arm in arm. They often played football together in the evenings. The day after he had kicked Brian's ball up into the yew tree, Eamonn climbed up to the very top of the tree, though it was slippery and dangerous because it was wet, and threw the ball down to Brian. That was after school, after all the others had gone home. On his way down the tree, a branch got caught between Eamonn's legs and he hurt himself in a funny way. The ball, however, was not burst, and that was the main thing. As they kicked it along the road, each of them dreamt of that glorious day when they would play football for the county. Brian never took his ball to school again.

At weekends, and sometimes in the evenings, he had to help his father scatter, foot and clamp the turf. When the summer holidays came, the turf was completely dry and ready to bring home. That's what Brian usually spent most of the long holidays at. Up early in the morning, he would tackle the donkey, fix the crates on the cart, and hit off for the bog at a cracking pace. The donkey was very lively in the morning, but by the end of the day his ears were wobbly and his tail limp. Passing the lake – at the end opposite the dangerous swally-hole – he often saw Fr. Smallhorn out in his rowboat, quietly fishing. If it was a warm day, Brian would go for a short dip in the cool water on his last trip home in the evening, just to get the dust out of his hair and ears and the corners of his eyes.

Most days he brought home six cartloads, but if he managed a seventh jag, his father would give him five euros. That last summer he only managed five a day. He almost had to force himself to return to the bog now. He wanted to be away from it, to turn his back on it, to forget it. Twilight was approaching as he closed the rusty bog gate behind him and shoved the bolt into the hole in the rotting gate-post for the last time on a Saturday evening in late August. He knew he would never go back. The bog was over. The only thing he would really miss was the lonely call of the curlew.

*   *   *

One day, at the beginning of September, the P.P., Fr. Smallhorn, called to see Mr. and Mrs. O'Brien and discuss what Brian was going to do, now that he had finished primary school. They had been expecting him. Brian was a good scholar and maybe he should go on to college, like

Patrick O'Connor. Mrs. O'Brien took the priest into the living-room for a cup of tea and gave Brian the beck to stay in the kitchen. There were a few things she and her husband wanted to bring up with the P.P. and it was better if Brian wasn't listening. But Brian sat close to the door in the kitchen and could hear most of what was being said.

Mr. O'Brien complained to the P.P. that Brian seemed to have lost interest in manual work of late. Mrs. O'Brien complained that he had withdrawn very much into himself over the past few months. Mrs. Heffernan had noticed it too. The priest made little comment. But they were both very proud, they said, that he had done so well in the Primary Cert. Then, to Brian's utter consternation, his mother said, out of the blue:

'Look, Father, I found this in his jeans the other day when I was washing them. There's something written on the first page but I don't know what it means. I was wondering if you could make any sense out of it. Maybe it's something important.'

Brian hadn't even missed his diary.

The P.P. read the two entries: ATWARTWOTITS and TWOBIRDS. He flipped through the diary and spotted O'Toole's poem inside the back cover, which Mrs. O'Brien hadn't noticed and Brian had never read. It went:

> Said the Father man
> To his teacher, 'Nan,
> I've a heifer and a bull.
> But the heifer, Nan,
> Can't stand her man,
> 'Cause his horn's too small to bull.

There was a very long silence. Brian was terrified in case he'd be called in to explain. He wanted to leave the kitchen, but he couldn't move. His legs were too weak.

Finally Fr. Smallhorn said:

'An extraordinary document, Mr. and Mrs. O'Brien, a

34

truly extraordinary document.'

He paused.

'Tell me,' he said, 'does your son do a lot of reading?'

'Only his schoolbooks, as far as we know,' said Mr. O'Brien.

'Does he write poems?'

'Poems? Not that we know of,' said Mrs. O'Brien. 'Why?'

'I'll explain in a minute,' said the P.P.

Then, holding the little white diary in his joined hands, and fixing his eyes on a pansy that formed part of the beautiful pattern of flowers in the little hearthrug that Mrs. O'Brien had woven when she was laid up with her bad leg in spring, he said:

'There's another little question I'd like to ask, but please don't be offended by it and don't get me wrong. I know it's ridiculous, basically, but I have to ask it. I have to be one hundred percent sure.'

There was a short pause. Tension mounted.

'Your son Brian – there's no doubt in the world, sure there isn't, that he's your very own son?'

Mr. O'Brien swallowed hard before his mouth fell open. His wife blushed deeply and looked away.

There was another long pause. The tension increased. Then Mr. O'Brien blurted out:

'Of course he's our son! If he's not our son, whose is he?'

'Yes, yes,' said the P.P., 'I knew it was a ridiculous question, but I had to ask it. You see, it's like this. A long time ago, when I was a student in Maynooth, a young man from Co. Tyrone wrote a famous book. His name was Flann O'Brien.'

'Never heard of him. No relation of ours,' said Mr. O'Brien gruffly.

'No doubt, no doubt,' said the priest, 'the north of

Ireland is far away. But he had a lot of relations in the North. Now the funny thing is, though, that his real name was not O'Brien at all, but O'Nolan.'

Mrs. O'Brien, somewhat flustered, said:

'What in God's name are you talking about, Father? I have no notion what you're trying to get at! What have we to do with a Mr. O'Nolan from Northern Ireland?'

'The famous book that that Mr. O'Nolan wrote was called *At Swim-Two-Birds*.'

'What was it called?' asked Mrs. O'Brien.

'*At Swim-Two-Birds*. Not an easy book to read.'

'I still don't get it,' said Mr. O'Brien. 'Why are you telling us all this?'

Fr. Smallhorn opened the soiled diary at the first page and handed it to them.

'Take a very close look at what your son has written!'

They looked and looked.

'What was the name of that book again, Father?' asked Mrs. O'Brien.

'*At Swim-Two-Birds*.'

Fr. Smallhorn could see the light dawning on them. Mr. O'Brien's mouth fell open again, Mrs. O'Brien's lips were tight and bloodless.

ATWARTWOTITS: AT-WAR-TWO-TITS.

TWOBIRDS: TWO-BIRDS.

'Now,' said the priest, 'take a look at what's inside the back cover.'

They bumped their heads together as they got closer to read O'Toole's poem. They were astonished, scandalized, embarrassed in front of Fr. Smallhorn.

'Now you know why I asked you those questions' said the priest. 'As you are well aware, you have a neighbour with a stiff member who is called O'Nolan.'

Brian remembered Mr. O'Nolan's strange way of talking and the funny way he had called his mother

36

'Sweetie' outside the house.

Fr. Smallhorn shook his head slowly.

'I'm afraid, Mr. and Mrs. O'Brien,' he said, 'what's in your son's diary is nothing but coded, unmitigated, un-hyphenated scatology. He's heading the wrong way. Flann O'Brien's book is beyond his ken, and as there is obviously no known relationship between your son and that revered author, the explanation for these obscenities is not to be found in his genes.'

'But that's where I found it,' said Mrs. O'Brien, misin-terpreting.

'Too big for his boots,' mumbled Mr. O'Brien, 'too bloody big for his boots! Excuse the language, Father.'

Bewildered, misunderstood once again, feeling totally alienated, Brian now got up, grabbed his football boots and was leaving the kitchen by the back door when he heard the P.P. say:

'Mr. and Mrs. O'Brien, I have no doubt your son knows all about the birds and the bees. My advice to you is that you send him to Nathy's. I went there myself. For boys only. They'll knock the corners off him there, I can assure you! That's what he needs! A good boarding-school.'

'And that's what I'd love,' Brian thought to himself, as he set off with his football to find Eamonn Maloney. 'Nathy's have a great team. And I hope they do Latin there, too.'

When he got out on the road he gave the ball a mighty kick up in the air. The P.P. went away, wheeling his bicycle. Another puncture. Through the sitting-room window Brian could see his parents arguing fiercely. He was glad to get away.

'And it's over the bar, the winning point for Roscommon!'

Up Roscommon!

JUST TALK

Q for Quebec had changed hands many times. It was twelve noon on a soft Monday in July when the new owner of the shop at the crossroads moved in. A week later there was nobody in the whole parish who did not know that Mr. Dumphries was a dummy.

He hadn't said a single word to Pat the Post when he brought him a small parcel the day after he arrived, and another one on the following Friday. At the butcher's on Wednesday he had simply pointed to the lamb chops in the window and when, after waiting in vain for a spoken order, Mrs. Connolly suggested a pound, maybe, might be the right thing, he only nodded. When people greeted him he made no reply and when the girl from the post office rang him and asked if he wanted to keep on Leclerque's telephone number, he just listened to her and said nothing, so she had to hang up again.

When he came to Quinn's supermarket in the rain that first Monday evening he attracted no special attention. Michael Quinn, the busy store manager, happening to raise his head from some precise end-of-the-day calculations, gave him no more than a casual glance as he passed his booth in grey tweed suit, grey shirt, grey spotted tie and black leather shoes. He pushed his trolley carefully and with deliberation up one passageway and down the next, looking closely at the articles on the shelves and nimbly stepping aside to let busy housewives pass, if he happened to be blocking a vital route. At the Pet's Food he took a packet of birdseed from the shelf and placed it in the trolley. From the Electrical Goods he took a 50-ft. roll of flex. At the far end of the store he added a bottle of milk from the Refrigerated Goods and started to wend his way back to the exit, scrutinising every sector as he passed. While standing in line at the check-out, he added a packet of Wrigley's to his purchases.

'Nice evening now, isn't it?' said the friendly girl at the cash, too mesmerized by the endless flow of goods and too bemused by the day-long flicking and clicking of the scanner to notice that it was, in fact, a bad evening. Nor did she notice that Mr. Dumphries made no reply. As he was waiting for the change out of his crisp €50 note Lizzie, the packing girl, put the seed, the milk, the flex and the chewing gum into a rustling plastic bag for him. But Mr. Dumphries indicated he wanted the milk, the flex and the birdseed separated, so she took them out again and put them in separate bags.

'Bye, sir,' she said, handing him the plastic bags and adding under her breadth, but not caring too much whether he heard her or not, 'finicky oul' eejit, whoever you are!'

It was Pat the Post who first discovered, on the Tuesday morning, that the new owner of Q for Quebec was a dummy. Leaning his bike against the garden wall, Pat rummaged in the big grey postbag slung across his shoulder and took out the little parcel addressed to Jerome Dumphries Esq., Q for Quebec, Castletownmore, Co. Roscommon. He walked up to the door and pressed the bell. Jerome promptly appeared.

'Good morning, Mr. Dumphries,' said Pat, 'not a bad day, now. Got a little parcel for you. Feels like a book or something.'

Jerome took the parcel and carefully undid the wrapping with his long, sensitive fingers.

'Were you expecting a book?' Pat asked, trying to open a conversation. Mr. Dumphries did not reply, but stood clasping firmly in his hands the yellow and blue *Teach Yourself French* manual.

'Will you soon be opening up again?' Pat inquired of the newcomer to his rounds.

Mr. Dumphries flicked tenderly through the pages of his new book, seeming not to hear.

'Well, he can't be deaf,' Pat thought to himself, 'he answered the doorbell pretty quick.'

Mr. Dumphries then put his hand in his trousers pocket, took out three coins and gave them to Pat. Pat was about to thank the decent man when he suddenly produced a padded yellow envelope from the inside pocket of his jacket and, pointing to the top right-hand corner of the envelope, indicated that he wanted Pat to put a stamp on it and post it for him.

'Well, normally I only deliver the post, not collect it' said Pat, 'but seeing as you're new here and don't know your way round yet, there's nothing like being obliging.'

Mr. Dumphries had turned his back and was disappearing into the house again.

'Good luck, and have a nice day,' was Pat's parting shot. He jumped on his bike and pedalled off down the road, whistling like a thrush but thinking hard about the quiet man at Quebec and the tip he didn't give him.

Pat had a letter for Molly Lavin from the daughter in Philadelphia.

'She's a great girl for writing,' Pat said, scattering the chickens from around the front door and walking straight into Lavin's kitchen. 'It isn't four weeks since you last heard from her.'

Molly quickly dropped the Rhode Island Red she held between her knees and was about to kill for the dinner. The chicken went squawking and floundering out the door into freedom. Brushing the feathers off her cardigan and giving a slight tug to her bedraggled skirt, she recovered her dignity, which had been temporarily ruffled by Pat's unceremonious entry.

'You're dead right: three weeks and five days, to be exact.'

'Maybe she's coming for Christmas,' said Pat.

'That'd be great news indeed,' said Molly, roughly opening the flimsy airmail letter with her strong thumbnail. She started reading the letter. It was fairly short, Pat could see. He waited, examining her face for some sign of drama as she read. He'd been a postman for over thirty years, and some people said he knew what was in most letters before they were opened. It was even rumoured that he himself had once penned a Christmas card to deaf old Bill McCoggan who had been expecting word from his son in England every day but hadn't heard from him in years.

'Well,' he said, when she'd finished, 'is she coming?'

'Indeed she's not. It's something else!'

Molly's face was clouded.

'Oh, I hope there's nothing wrong!'

'Nothing wrong, nothing right,' she said, waiting for Pat to drag it out of her.

'Would she be ill now?'

'You're near enough to it,' said Mrs. Lavin, as she started to put the letter back in the violated envelope. 'She's sick alright – but in the head!'

'What's up then?' said Pat, with rising curiosity.

'She's getting married,' said Molly, 'and you'd never guess to what!'

'To a man, no doubt,' said Pat.

'To a black,' said Mrs. Lavin, 'and to crown it all, she's already expecting a baby. She must be gone mad! What'll the neighbours say when they hear this?'

'Sure how will the neighbours know,' said Pat, 'if you don't tell them yourself? I, for one, won't say a word about it, and you could tell your worst sins to your new neighbour up the road there and he'd never say a word about it either.'

'Who's that?' asked Molly. 'What do you mean?'

'Silent Night. Didn't you know? It's only July, but Christmas is here already. Silent Night is in the Q.'

Now it was Pat's turn to wait.

'What in God's name are you blathering about?' said Mrs. Lavin. 'Have you gone off your head altogether?'

Pat, with years of experience behind him, was enjoying the drama and the delights of gradual denouement.

'A dummy,' he said, has moved into Leclerque's place. He's learning French but he can't speak. Jasus, did you ever!' he said, and let out a mighty laugh. 'Wonders never cease!'

He went out, leaving behind a confused Mrs. Lavin. He threw his leg across the bar and off he went, whistling as usual. At the presbytery he handed the newspaper from England to the disappointed P.P.'s housekeeper who had been peeping from behind the curtains in the high-ceilinged living room for half an hour, hoping that today's post might have a letter from her divorced brother in the North, or at least a card with palm trees and a blue sky from a parishioner holidaying in Ibiza or Malibu, instead of the usual appeal letters from the St. Vincent de Paul Society and missionary magazines with the black babies on the cover. As Pat was dropping Mr. Dumphries' little padded letter into the green P&T post-box outside Bill Meaney's pub, he happened to glance at the address: Mr. Dumphries, Q for Quebec, Castletownmore. 'Sweet Holy Christ!' said Pat out loud, 'writin' to himself! The poor auld devil must be awfully lonesome. But sure I suppose if normal people talk to themselves, why shouldn't a dummy write to himself?'

He stepped nimbly into the pub to deliver the un-welcome garda summons ('That'd be for staying open after hours last Saturday week, Bill') and to savour to the full with Frank the barman over a pint of Guinness the delightful snippets of confidential news he had gathered on his morning's round.

The next day, Wednesday, Mr. Dumphries returned to the supermarket. Taking from his breast pocket a leather-bound notebook with a small white pen in it, he started his shopping. The notebook was thick and full of precisely written notes in a fine hand, doubly underlined in places and highlighted with a yellow marker. On the last page there was a shopping list and now Jerome passed among the shelves, ticking off the numbered items one after the other down the list. He placed each article with delibera-tion in the trolley and he did not have to retrace his steps once before arriving at the cash. Then he snapped the small, white pen back in the notebook and paid in silence for the goods, which quick Lizzy sorted into three bags according to category. He smiled, took the bags out to the car, loaded them onto the back seat, started the pale blue Ford and headed for the Q.

At that very same time Julia O'Grady was taking a rest on the parapet of the bridge out the road around Cooney's Corner. Talking to herself as usual, the drop she had taken was making the going tough. It was still a mile and a half home, and if she couldn't go any faster the greasy fish and chips would be stone cold by the time Martin got them. But good enough for him anyway and he sat in the corner most of the day complaining, when she was near, about the pain in his shoulder and his bowels that hadn't moved for a week, and waiting for the TV to come on in the evening and hoping nobody in the parish would die in case he'd have to get up off his arse and dig another grave and earn an extra tenner. She cursed and blinded when the bald-headed Mick Rannigan flew by in his smoky old bone-shaker. Since they won a bit of money in the crossword and

43

bought the old Morris, Mick and the wife had started going straight down the middle aisle on Sundays, though everyone knew they had hardly spoken to each other for five years and the P.P. had to come out to them only last week because Mick had tried to poison Kate and the tongue swelled up in her head and she couldn't say the Rosary, but Dr. Kelly only found a small fish-bone stuck in her gullet and assured her as he was removing it that she'd be as eloquent as Demosthenes again within a week. 'Bad cess to them motor-cars,' Julia cursed, but hope swelled in her breast again when the blue Ford came sweeping around the corner. Desperately she waved Mr. Dumphries down and couldn't believe her luck when the car came to a halt.

'Would you take me a bit of the way with you, sir?' she asked, getting in beside the stranger before he could reply.

'Jasus, wait,' she said, fumbling out again, 'me fish and chips, I left them on the bridge!'

Before she got back in Mr. Dumphries had switched on the cassette recorder. A little red light glowed unnoticed on the dashboard.

'Drive on, James,' she said, relaxing in the passenger seat and glancing sideways at the stranger to see if he appreciated her little pleasantry. She liked the phrase herself the first time her niece from England used it to the taximan at the station.

'Isn't it bad weather we're having for July,' she said. 'It'll be hard to get the turf dry if it continues like this.'

She threw an eye at the grey tweeds and black, leather shoes.

'But you're hardly a farmer yourself, I'd say. And right you are. It's only a fool's job. It's the bit of education that counts. Everybody should be made stick to their books. There's my old man and he can only talk about pigs and sheep and since we got the TV he doesn't talk to me at all. Meself, I was good at books when I was at school and I

44

like an intelligent conversation with people who are smart. Watch out, be God! Them's Jimmy O Brien's sheep. They must've broke out again. Why that lazy good-for-nothin' doesn't do a bit of fencin' I'll never know.'

Mr. Dumphries had to slow down almost to a standstill to let the sheep pass. The border collie lay respectfully at the edge of the road, keeping a close eye on the animals while the car crept by. Then a low whistle from Jimmy, who had come out a gap and was trying to round up the sheep, sent the dog about his unerring task of organizing the recalcitrant woollies and getting them all back into the fold they had wantonly strayed from.

Julia looked for the window handle, but there was none.

'Funny bloody car,' she said to herself, 'can't even open the windows!'

Mr. Dumphries pressed a button on his side and down went the glass. Julia couldn't believe it. Then she called out proudly:

'Hello, Jimmy! The sheep givin' trouble again?'

'Ara, is it yourself, Julia? I didn't recognize ye.'

'How's the old man?'

Mr. Dumphries had gathered speed again and they were almost out of earshot as Jimmy replied.

'On his last legs, I'm afraid. Don't think he'll last another night.'

'Good,' muttered Julia to herself, as the window went up again. 'That's another tenner, maybe.'

They approached Q for Quebec.

'You can let me out at the crossroads,' she said to the driver, 'if you're goin' straight on. I've only another half a mile or so down the side road, though me feet are killin' me and I wouldn't mind ridin' in your lovely car straight to the front door. That's the Q now,' she said, no one in it since that Leclerque fella with the funny way of talkin' closed it down two weeks ago and went off back to Canada or Australia or wherever he came from. I could never understand a word he was sayin', but he had everythin' in his little shop and I never had to go into town for a bit of butter or a stamp but only to collect the pension of a Friday. But come to think of it now, I did hear in Quinn's today that some kind of a dummy from Germany with a funny second name has moved in.'

Mr. Dumphries came to a gentle halt.

'Look,' said Julia, 'at the sign Leclerque put up in the window when he was leavin': SHUTTING UP. I hope the new owner soon takes it down and puts up OPENING UP or I'll be spendin' the rest o' me born days like a tramp on the roads.'

She got out, reluctantly, when Mr. Dumphries switched off the engine.

'Thanks for the lift anyway,' she said and headed off unsteadily down the bye-road, gallantly pushing the fish and chips up under her gansy for protection against the light rain that was just beginning to fall. Hoping against hope that the gentleman might take pity on her, she looked behind her only to see the car still parked there and Mr. Dumphries entering the front door with the parcels. A yellow wink flashed from the car as he locked it with his electronic key.

'A God no,' she said. 'Don't tell me that's Jerry. Well, well, wait till Martin hears this. The new shopkeeper from Germany gave me a lift all the way from town. A very nice man, an' easy to talk to. An intelligent man, and dressed beautifully. God, I hope I didn't say anything wrong.'

She went on down the road, talking to herself. Her head felt light and her legs heavy, what with the fresh air and the drop of Jameson's and the excitement of the car ride and the nice man she had had the conversation with.

'And he hasn't a trace of an accent,' she said to Martin, as she walked in the front door.

Known at the beginning of the week as Jerome Dumphries, Esq., the new owner of Q for Quebec quickly became Mr. Jerome Dumphries, then Jerome Dumphries, then Jerome and finally Jerry the Dummy. Word went round very fast that in contrast to the garrulous Mr. Leclerque, whom everybody found so hard to understand, his successor couldn't speak at all. For that very reason, for the purpose of establishing his identity and his intentions, close observation of his outward appearance, his activities, his body language, his habits, his contacts became the occupation, the duty in fact, of everybody in Castletownmore. Rumours began to spread. As his car had a Dublin registration, he must be a civil servant. Around fifty, he probably had retired early because of his impediment. On the other hand, with his grey tweed suit and his notebook and his birdseed and his methodological approach to shopping, he might well be a scientist, perhaps an ornithologist. Or maybe he was the son of a German spy, come to track down Leclerque for some heinous crime his father had committed when he was in the French Resistance, but Leclerque got the wind of it in time and skedaddled. That's why Jerry was learning French. The suggestion was even made that he wasn't dumb at all, but only pretending.

Support for the latter theory, though secret, came from a completely unexpected quarter. The P.P. was relaxing after lunch in his plush easy chair, his slippered feet resting on the low footstool, when Mary brought in the newspaper from England. She placed it quietly on the magazine rack beside his dozing reverence. She lowered the blinds a little, spread an embroidered linen cloth on the small, round side table and tiptoed back to the kitchen. Half an hour later she returned with the same cup, saucer, spoon, sugar-bowl, milk-jug and coffee-pot that she had brought him at that time every day for the past 15 years. At the beginning she had had difficulty in making the coffee to his taste – tea she would have had no trouble with – but when he showed her how to grind the coffee beans and explained to her how the percolator worked and told her the exact amount of coffee required to get the precise flavour he had got used to during his years in Surrey as a curate, she caught on quickly enough. The only time in all those years that the P.P. came closer than a metre to his housemaid was that morning when he initiated her into the mysteries of coffee-making.

'Coffee, Father,' she announced gently.

The P.P. reacted with a slight jolt as he emerged from his doze. He dismissed his faithful servant with a circumspect 'Thank you, Mary', secretly fearing he might even have been snoring when she came in. He poured some coffee into the china cup and added a little milk, but immediately small clotted curds appeared on the surface. He called after Mary.

'It's gone sour,' he said, handing her the milk jug.

'I'm sorry, Father!' she said.

Highly embarrassed, she hurried out to get a fresh supply, taking the spoiled beverage with her.

While he was waiting, Fr. O'Rourke opened the newspaper and, as usual, went straight to the cricket results. Delighted that Guildford had won the Surrey League, he turned over the next page. His attention was immediately caught by a bold headline which read: Catholic Priest A Paedophile. He hurriedly read through the article. He was moved by a sincere sorrow for the scandal which would be caused if it was really true. Did such things actually happen? he asked himself. Somehow he just could not believe it. He had never come across a single case. Being a practical man, he would only accept what he knew to be true. As Mary returned with fresh milk, he turned quickly over to the international news page.

'Thank you, Mary, thank you. Are my shoes ready?'

He drank his coffee quickly. Then he stood up and folded the newspaper away, being careful to remove the offensive page and throw it in the wastepaper basket. He put on his black leather shoes, took his walking-stick and his breviary and set out on his usual afternoon walk. He headed in the direction of Q for Quebec. He had heard there was a strange civil servant living there now, who was of German extraction, liked Christmas carols but couldn't talk. He wondered if he was a Catholic. If he was, how could he hear his confessions? He had never had a parishioner like that before. Old Bill McCoggan was half deaf, but that was a different problem and in his theology days they had been taught how to deal with such cases. On the other hand, unless Jerry's people were from Bavaria, he was more likely to be a Protestant. He hooked his walking-stick on his arm, opened his breviary, and prayed as he went along. *Out of the depths I have cried unto Thee, O Lord.* But Fr. O'Rourke was ill at ease. He found no comfort today in the lovely rhythms of the psalms. *By the waters of Babylon, there we sat down.* He felt out of step with things. He passed Cooney's Corner and the bridge. No concentration. Just words on his lips, without meaning. *The Lord is my shepherd, there is nothing I shall want.* Should he drop in and see how old Andy O'Brien was? On the way back, perhaps. *Three boys in the fiery furnace.* Children of Sion. Children of Albion. Paedophile priests. It couldn't be! What was the world coming to? Just talk, that's all. Rumours and talk. He struggled on through vespers. He was coming to the crossroads. *As the hart panteth.* Suddenly, like an arrow through the air, the words came flying at him from the house, 'Pretty boy. Pretty boy.' He stopped dead, momentarily bewildered. He listened hard but he heard the words no more. Then recognition and recollection slowly broke in on his mind. Of course! A budgie. His English housekeeper had one when he was a curate in Guildford. So Jerry kept a budgie. Nothing strange about that. He reopened his breviary. Or was there? He walked on up the road, stopped and turned back. He wanted to be certain. Keeping his eye on the psalms and his ear on the house, he passed very close to the garden wall of Q for Quebec. Then he stopped dead again and almost dropped his walking stick. He couldn't believe his ears. There were other voices, human voices this time, a man's voice saying 'Wonders never cease', a woman's voice saying 'Sick in the head.' Did he not know those voices? He moved on a step or two and waited, but nothing more came. Certain of what he had heard but now more puzzled than ever, he made his way back, slowly at first but gathering speed as his thoughts began to buzz in his head. A German dummy. A talking bird. A silent civil servant. A voice telling of wonders. Silent. Silenced maybe, but not a dummy? The newspaper headline. The P.P. wondered. No, it couldn't be! Lost in thought, he soon found himself back again at the presbytery. He had quite forgotten to call on old Andy.

Fr. O'Rourke kept his thoughts to himself. Jerry continued to be the main topic of conversation up and down the parish. He was observed occasionally working in the garden, close to the ground inside the low front wall. He did not return to the supermarket for a long time. On the Friday, Pat the Post had another parcel for him, a padded yellow envelope which Jerry took quickly from him and went inside, in silence as usual. The light in the house was often seen burning late into the night and some of the farmers returning from the pub after closing hours swore they heard voices as they were passing. But nobody was ever seen entering or leaving. Around midday on Friday Jerry called to the butcher's again. On Fridays Mrs. Connolly always kept a supply of whiting and haddock, but Jerry pointed to the chops and this soon gave rise to the widespread conviction that he was definitely a Protestant. Tension began to mount at the weekend. If he was a Catholic, would Jerry go to confessions on Saturday evening or, more important still, would he turn up for Mass on Sunday? The parish was divided into two main camps on these issues. There were those who argued logically that a dummy couldn't go to confessions because he couldn't tell his sins to the priest. Others said that that was no hindrance: he could write them down and hand them in and beat his breast as a sign of contrition. Eugene Lavin recalled that he himself actually lost the talk once in the confessional but the priest gave him absolution anyway. But the more important issue was Mass on Sunday. Some were convinced that he would be there: wasn't he a civil servant and didn't he drive a Ford? The betting started. The heaviest wager was laid by Mrs. Connolly who, with the fish in mind, bet a straight €100 with Dr. Kelly that Jerry would not be there. Pat the Post laid €5 with John-Eddy, the tailor, that he would certainly be there, because all Irish civil servants had to be Catholics.

The blue Ford stayed where it was all Saturday evening. No confessions! But, lo and behold! At three minutes to eleven on the Sunday morning Jerry drove up in front of the church and parked his car ten metres from the main entrance, in the free space that everybody knew – though there was no sign up anywhere – was reserved for the P.P.'s Cortina when he got back from the out-church. He got out, straightened his tie, walked towards the high oak door, mounted the three steps up to the porch, put 50 cents on the collection table ("Thanks, me good man," said sacristan-cum-collector Luke) and entered the main body of the building. He proceeded straight down the centre aisle towards the altar, steadily, head erect, looking neither left nor right. And he prayed as he went along! Everybody could see his mouth and lips opening and closing rhythmically as he moved up the aisle. Whisperings and nudges and knowing glances went rippling through the congregation, that was tight-packed as always at the back, but grew less and less congested the closer to the altar. In the very front row there was never anyone now except Mick and Maisie Rannigan. With every step that Jerry took the tension mounted. Everybody hoped he wouldn't come into their row. But he kept on going – till he reached Andy O'Brien's coffin. Andy had passed away on the Friday evening and his remains had been brought to the church on the Saturday and the funeral was to take place after the 11 o'clock Mass on Sunday. Jerry stood with bowed head in front of the coffin for a moment, genuflected and moved into the seat beside Maisie Rannigan. Maisie, thinking first it was Mick because he had had to go off looking for somewhere to park the Morris, whispered to him out of the side of her mouth, 'Where did you get parking?' but she got no answer. She asked again, and annoyed that her husband was ignoring her once more in front of everyone, she turned to glower at him only to discover that Mick was Jerry. Maisie stiffened, almost panicked. If she could have got out of the seat she would have run away. She prayed that Mick would come soon. Just then the church bell struck 11. Jerry stood bolt upright. The rest of the congregation remained kneeling or sitting. They knew Mass never began before 10 past 11 – 'to accommodate the stragglers,' Fr. O'Rourke explained once. Maisie heard Mick coming up the aisle in his hob-nailed boots. She felt almost as happy as on the day she had married him in that same church 35 years before. When Mick got to the front row he tried to cross in in front of the unexpected intruder but Jerry, standing tall and firm like a lighthouse, wouldn't budge and the Rannigans had to accept being divorced by the silent imposter in front of the whole parish till Mass was over.

Today it was almost 20 past 11 when a rather flustered P.P. appeared on the altar. As he proceeded with the liturgy the attention of most of the faithful remained concentrated on Jerry. Would he join in the responses? If he couldn't talk, perhaps he could sing. Did he know the hymns? It was quickly noticed that he knew exactly when to stand up and when to kneel down. As he sat down for the sermon he quietly put his right hand inside his jacket above his heart. The action did not go unnoticed. He repeated it when the sermon was over. Palpitations? A coronary coming on? Never had a sermon of the P.P.'s fallen on such deaf ears. Apart from Jerry, nobody seemed to be listening. '"In my father's house there are many mansions." Words taken from the holy gospel according to St. John, Chapter 14, verse 2. My dear brethren! We all know only too well that life on this earth is a valley of tears.' Fr. O'Rourke was trying to offer consolation to the bereaved. 'Christ has gone before us to prepare an eternal dwelling for his faithful servants. And Andy O'Brien, as everybody here knows, was one of those faithful servants.' A little later came Fr. O'Rourke's application of the scripture passage to the modern world, his favourite device in interpreting the Bible: 'Death is not the end, it's only the beginning, for he who believes in Christ shall live forever. Beyond the grave another, a better, life awaits us. In heaven we will all have our own mansion, our own flat, our own car – if there are cars in heaven – and,' he added, glancing at Jerry, 'our own parking area.' Mick Rannigan nodded his head in complete approval. The P.P. kept his sermon short today: he could see the deaf ears.

Jerry prayed visibly right through Mass. He did not join in the hymns. When it came to the 'Peace be with you' he simultaneously gave his right hand to Maisie and his left hand to Mick, without turning his head, and raised them for a moment to the level of his shoulders. Then he dropped them again. No word. When Mass was over he stayed on in the church until Andy's remains were removed to Cloonree cemetery and everybody had left. Then he got up, went to his car and drove straight home to Q for Quebec.

*   *   *

The lounge in Meaney's pub had never been so full. The seven or eight small round tables were straining under the weight of Guinness glasses and Jameson glasses and Fanta glasses and occasional mineral-water glasses and over-full ash-trays (smoking not yet being outlawed). On each of the few backless stools that were spread around, two or three neighbourly mothers sat precariously back to back, with one leg on the ground for support, while small and not-so-small children climbed all over them demanding chips and ketchup. The red, plastic bench along the wall was occupied by old men and women, huddled close, calling to memory the many good deeds and occasional bad ones committed by old Andy, and secretly hoping it wouldn't be their turn next to go. The young and middle-aged were crowded around the bar, the mourners calling for rounds for relatives and neighbours and the three barmen engaged in a fierce flurry of glass-washing, money-counting, order-taking, pint-pulling. Lizzy, the packing-girl, was helping out. As the alcohol levels rose, the buzz of conversation got louder and louder. The voluntary silence to which the mourning community had subjected itself at the funeral out of respect for the dead and the bereaved, now gave way to a flood of talk that seemed to be all the more spirited for the temporary restraint imposed upon its natural flow. As the temperature in the room rose, the pallid faces and stiff lips of the graveside softened into rounder lines and ruddier hues. Old Andy had been very popular and they were determined to bury him dacent.

But there was a second reason for the record crowd in Meaney's pub that Sunday, and it wasn't the match in Croke Park: out of respect for the dead, the TV wasn't even switched on. Consciously or subconsciously, everybody wanted to hear or take part in a post mortem on Jerry. It was little Dr. Kelly who set the ball rolling. Perched up on his high stool at the end of the bar, he spotted Mrs. Connolly chatting to Mrs. Lavin. With a broad smile on his face, he called out to her across the lounge:

'Fish or flesh, Mrs. Connolly?'

'Okay, Doc,' she said, making her way over to him and placing two €50 notes on the counter in front of him. 'You win. I was wrong – for once in me life. Here you are, your pound of flesh.' She always used this little bon mot with the educated doctor when he came for his lamb chops on Saturday mornings. She herself had been a boarder with the Ursulines in Sligo, but left after the Inter Cert to marry her butcher boy.

'I hope you don't mind me asking, Doc,' she said, 'but has Jerry been to see you? They're saying, you know, that he has a bad heart.'

'No, Mrs. Connolly. He hasn't said a word to me about it,' said the doctor, tongue in cheek. 'What are you having?'

Pat the Post came up to them, a broad smile on his face, too.

'Such a devout Catholic I never seen in me life!' he said. 'A sure winner right from the start. John-Eddy won't like having to cough up his fiver!'

The tailor didn't turn up for Mass that Sunday.

Scenting that free drinks might be going, Maisie Rannigan and Julia O'Grady elbowed their way through to the bar.

'That was a fine grave Martin dug for Andy,' said the

doctor.

'Didn't he deserve it?' said Julia. A nicer neighbour you couldn't find.'

'Let's drink on that,' said the doctor. 'Lizzie, five small ones.'

'You have a few other nice neighbours, too, Julia,' said Pat the Post. 'Sure you couldn't meet a more upright, dacent, holy man than your German.'

'I'm not so sure about that,' said Mrs. Connolly.

'Why not?' chuckled the doctor.

'Good Catholics don't eat meat on Fridays.'

'Arrah, that's all a thing of the past since the Council,' said Pat. 'Didn't you see the way he behaved in church? There in good time, no gawkin' about him!'

'Yes,' said Maisie, 'and occupying the poor P.P.'s parking space with his fancy car. Fr. O'Rourke was right to give him the dig.'

'Did you not notice him praying?' said Pat, feeling a great necessity to defend Jerry's orthodoxy on account of the good luck he had brought him. 'He never stopped whispering prayers to the Almighty all during Mass! You ought to know, Maisie, you were right beside him.'

Lizzie brought them their drinks and remained at the counter for a few moments, listening to the conversation.

'Prayers is it?' said Maisie, 'prayers!' She emptied her glass of whiskey in one gulp, to help her achieve the dramatic force that the revelation she was about to make deserved.

'Prayers!' she said again. 'Let me tell you all one thing and one thing only: that man is an unholy, irreverent bastard. He's not a Catholic at all!'

'What do you mean?' asked Mrs. Connolly, with great interest.

'Wrigley's,' said Maisie.

'Is that his real name?' Julia asked.

'Wrigley's chewing gum, you googeen,' said Maisie. 'And if anyone doesn't believe me, ask my Mick. He was the other side of him.'

'Well, now, that's very interesting,' said Lizzy, and went back to her work washing up the glasses.

'That proves nothing' said Pat, determined to defend Jerry to the bitter end.

Over near the door that led out onto the street Mrs. O'Brien had quickly occupied the half-seat vacated by Mrs. Connolly. Martin O'Grady was sat comfortably at the end of the bench beside them, communing in some mysterious way with Sam, the old pub collie, and hoping they might switch on the TV. The mud and grime of the cemetery had caked on his wellingtons and his hands were blistered and sore, but the tenner he got for the grave would keep him in fish and chips for a long time, and Julia could have her dropeen when she went shopping, and she wouldn't be nagging him again for another while anyway. Valiant efforts to throw more light on the enigmatic Mr. Dumphries were now forthcoming from this side of the pub.

'I've heard them say he's a great man for Christmas carols,' said Mrs. Lavin.

'If he is,' said Martin, 'it's only puttin' on he is. Will I tell ye what I think? I think he's a bit of a skirt-chaser.' He had picked the word up from the TV. 'Julia told me he gave her a big, yellow wink after letting her out of the car.'

'If you ask me,' said Mrs. Lavin, finishing off her second pint, 'he's a step-dancer.'

'A step-dancer! How do you make that out?' asked Mrs. O'Brien.

'Don't tell me,' said Mrs. Lavin, her breast swelling with the confidence of a crown witness, 'that none of ye noticed the way he took Mick and Maisie's hands at the 'Peace be with you'! I was sure and certain he was going to do the three-hand-reel with them and was only waiting for the music to start.'

'He has the shoes of a dancer alright,' said Mrs. O'Brien.

'I think he might be a football coach,' contributed Mick Rannigan, thinking of the chewing gum.

'Well, he's a Catholic anyway, so he is,' said Martin, looking at the ground and getting off the uncomfortable topic of footwear, 'and that other little impediment that he has …'

Before he could finish his sentence, the door beside him opened and in stepped a tall, auburn-haired young woman nobody had ever seen before. She was wearing a blue blazer, a white striped blouse, and a red skirt with stars on it. She had a blue leather handbag over her left shoulder and her hands hung casually in the outside pockets of her blazer. Her shining black shoes had thick modern soles and heels, which made her look taller than she actually was. Martin instinctively pulled his legs in under the bench as she passed him. She made her way slowly through the crowd. As she approached the bar the hubbub of conversation gradually subsided, like an electric saw when it's switched off. All eyes, and ears, were on her.

'Excuse me, sir,' she said to Frank, the barman, who had his back to her washing glasses at the sink.

He didn't hear her at first.

'Sir,' she repeated, 'excuse me.'

Frank turned.

'I wonder could you help me, sir. I'm looking for accommodation. Is there a hotel in the vicinity?'

'No, mam,' said Frank. 'there isn't. The nearest hotel is in Roscommon.'

'And how far away might Roscommon be?'

'About 50 kilometres, mam.'

'Oh, that's rather a distance.'

'Well, if you wouldn't mind B&B, you might try Mrs. Lynch at the end of the village. She's sure to have a room free. Not many tourists pass through Castletownmore, you know. Will I give her a buzz?'

'That would be very kind of you, I'm sure.'

Frank took his mobile out of his hip pocket and retired to the back room where it was quieter.

'Will you be staying a while?' Doc Kelly ventured to ask her, while she was waiting.

'Indefinitely,' she answered, 'it depends on how successful I am in my quest.'

'And,' pursued Doc, knowing she wanted to be asked, 'what are you in quest of?'

'Ancestors,' she replied, 'I'm trying to track down where my forefathers came from.'

Frank returned.

'No problem, mam. Mrs. Lynch has a great big double room with a TV and a phone and you can stay there as long as you like.'

'Gee, that's delightful! You're so kind. Now perhaps if you could give me directions as to how to get to Mrs. Lynch's, I'll be on my way.'

She spoke so nicely and in such soft, pleasant tones that gentle emotions began to stir in the hearts of the bachelors standing about, or re-kindled in the memories of men long married.

'It's just up the road there, you don't need any directions at all,' said Pat the Post, plucking up courage.

She turned to go.

'Are you in a big hurry?' said Doc Kelly. 'Remember, when God made time, he made plenty of it. Stay for a while and have a drink with us.'

The men could have clapped the doctor on the back. They held their breaths, waiting for her response, and when she shrugged her lovely shoulders as if to say, 'I'm in no great hurry, really', at least five voices rang out in chorus, 'What are you having?' The women's reaction was less enthusiastic.

'Oh, you're all so generous,' she said. 'Let me see. I'd love a shandy, I'm rather thirsty after the long drive.'

'You're from Dublin, I suppose, Miss....' said Mrs. Connolly.

'Ms. Wolf-Butler. But please, just call me Mary, plain Mary. No, I'm not from Dublin – much further away.'

'Do you hear Connolly making a fool of herself?' whispered Mrs. Lavin to Mrs. O'Brien in the background. Sure anyone would know that's not an Irish accent.'

Lizzy brought the shandy.

'Cheers!'

'To your health!'

'Welcome to Ireland!'

'Sláinte!'

'Did your people come from Castletownmore?' asked Doc Kelly.

'That's what I'm here to investigate. I'm not sure. You see, on my father's side I'm German – that's the wolfish element in me! – but my mother's people were Butlers who emigrated to Providence, Rhode Island, in the late forties. From old letters and photographs I gather that they came from somewhere in the west of Roscommon county. They owned a little shop, I believe. Look, I've got a photo.'

As many as could gathered around to look at the photo and at the same time get a little closer to the interesting visitor. Conversation began to gather momentum again among those who were further back from the front line. Snippets of what was said at the bar were relayed to those who were out of earshot, amplified with appropriate comments and constructive interpretations, and increasing in inaccuracy the further they got from the source.

Alert as ever, it was Pat the Post who first recognized the shop at the crossroads.

'Q for Quebec!' he announced triumphantly.

'What does that mean?' Mary asked.

'That's the name of the shop now,' Pat said. 'That's what Mr. Leclerque called it. It has changed hands a lot o' times. But now that I think of it, I remember me father tellin' me it was once owned by a Paddy Butler who went off to the States to make his fortune in the fifties. Things were bad then, mam.'

'I can't believe it!' she said. 'My grandfather's name was Paddy Butler. Wonderful! Brilliant! I've hit the bull's eye straightaway. I must get out there and have a talk with the people in my ancestral home. Who's in the shop now?'

'You're out o' luck. It's closed down,' Julia announced curtly.

'Oh, no!' said Mary, visibly disappointed.

'Bad cess to the new one who's in it,' added Julia, enjoying the limelight, 'I wished he'd open it up again. It's an awful long way into town on your pins. Not that I'm sayin' anythin' bad about the man. He's a real gentleman.'

'Well, I'm sure I can go and have a look around the old place in any case,' Mary said. 'And why waste time? I'll drive out there right now and have a talk with this Mr. Leclerque. Can anyone give me directions?'

'I'll show you where it is,' Julia volunteered, 'I live out that way. Come on, I was about to go home anyway.'

Julia caught Mary by the arm and started ushering her towards the door. If looks could kill, Julia would not have reached the door alive.

'But Leclerque's gone...'

'There's a German dummy...'

'He won't have much to say to you...'

Mary was no longer listening.

'I'll be back tomorrow evening,' she said over her

shoulder, and vanished out the door with Julia.

Hardly had the tension about Jerry's uncertain attendance at Mass relaxed when a new form of speculation took its place: would Mary come back, or would they never see her again in the pub? And once more the betting started. Mrs. Connolly was more careful this time. She would only bet €5 with the doctor that there would be no return. Pat the Post, thinking the same, would go doubles or quits with John-Eddy. Now that Julia wasn't about, Martin said he'd put his tenner on Mary to return and Frank the barman took him up on it.

'She's gone,' said Frank, 'and that's it.'

'Begod I don't think you're right there, Frank,' said young Paul Lavin, letting his hopes determine his judgement. 'She won't get much out of Jerry, I'm thinkin', so she'll be back to see if we can tell her any more about the Butlers.'

When the sergeant appeared in the doorway, and Bill Meaney started calling out with great urgency, 'Time up now, lads, the holy hour has started', they all got a move on. He still hadn't paid the first fine and he didn't want to get on the wrong side of sergeant Scally again. When everybody had left, the sergeant himself ordered a pint, having every reason to expect it would be on the house.

'Who was that Julia was with in the car?' he asked Bill. 'She had a Dublin registration so I pulled her for speeding. She was fairly tipping it around Cooney's corner.'

'Christ, you didn't,' said Bill. 'That's the end of her, then. She's an innocent young girl from America trying to find out about her ancestors. She's related, it seems, to the Butlers who used to run the shop at the crossroads in the forties. She's gone out to see if Silent Night can give her any information. Can't imagine Jerry'll detain her too long! Can you? There'll be great crack tomorrow evening when she comes back – if she does come back!"

Monday was normally a slack day, but that evening the pub started filling up around half past seven. The farmers finished work a bit early, it being a bad day anyway. Some were wearing their Sunday clothes again. Many of the women came back, too, not feeling too sure why the had got dressed up. Mrs. Lavin was wearing a necklace she hadn't put on for years. Unusual odours of birthday-present perfumes mixed with the more customary smell of Guinness and cigarette ash. Sergeant Scally, off duty, sat quietly in a corner. The conversation at first was general, the weather, as usual, being the main topic, followed in second place by the football results. But Mary was in everybody's mind. In different ways. Johnny Molloy, who always got things wrong, only half heard about her quest for her ancestors and thought she was looking for her sister Anne. Bill McCoggan, deaf in the right ear, was convinced she was there to hunt wolves. Somehow Mrs. Lavin, hearing of Rhode Island, couldn't help associating her with the chicken she had killed for lunch. And Paul Carroll, misinterpreting Providence, could swear he heard her say she was sent to them by the Almighty Himself. For Paul Lavin she was simply divine anyway. Doc Kelly concocted his own version for the benefit of Frank the barman.

'So you don't think Queen Mary will be coming back, Frank?'

'Why Queen Mary?' Frank asked.

'Didn't she make a knight of you, Frank? I distinctly heard her say 'Sir' to you three times. Only a queen can do that. Sir Frank, the Knight of the frothy pint!'

It was coming up ten o'clock, and Mrs. Connolly was beginning to feel her luck had turned and she would recuperate some of her losses. Martin O'Grady, on the other hand, was growing more and more despondent. If he lost the tenner, he might as well start digging a grave for himself, for he'd never hear the end of it from Julia. Frank switched on the TV and they were half way through the ten o'clock news when Sam gave a short bark, the door opened, and back came Mary again.

A loud cheer went up, drowning out the few moans. A corridor opened automatically before her as she made her way through the crowd to the bar on an invisible red carpet.

'Switch off that bloody – excuse me – that television, will you, Frank,' Paul Lavin said, 'I'm dyin' to hear the news from Mary.'

'And quite an amount of news there is, too,' said Mary.

'A shandy first to wet your whistle?' Mick Corcoran, the pig-dealer, suggested agriculturally.

'Tell us, did you meet Jerry?' asked the Doc, with a mischievous smile on his lips.

'Do you mean Mr. Dumphries? I thought you told me his name was Leclerque.'

The misunderstanding was soon cleared up.

'Oh yes,' she said, 'I had a very long chat with him. A most interesting person! A real nice English gentleman!'

They pressed around her, not believing their ears, certain that there was another misunderstanding.

'Keep back a bit,' Paul said, trying chivalrously to protect her from being crushed against the counter.

'Did you…say,' said Pat the Post, hardly able to formulate the question, 'that… he talked... to you!'

'Of course he did,' she said, 'why shouldn't he?'

'But he can't talk, he's… he's…'

'A dummy,' Mick Rannigan finished it for him.

'A dummy! Wherever did you get that notion? I could hardly get away from him, he had so much to say. He knew nothing about my ancestors but he seems to know an awful lot about what's going on in Castletownmore.'

'Like what?' Mick asked.

'He told me, for instance, that the pastor gets a newspaper from England every day, and that the owner of the pub here got a fine for not obeying the licensing laws, and that the daughter of a certain Mrs. Lavin is expecting a baby by a black man in America, and that...'

Shock waves rippled through the lounge. Mouths opened wide, and wider, as more details were revealed. The astonishment was unbounded. Everybody was dumbfounded. Then Mrs. Lavin, the first to recover, gave a loud shriek and flew straight at Pat the Post, her arms flailing about her like the wings of a fighting bantam cock.

'Hold on, wait a minute,' said Pat, trying to defend his face as he glanced with suspicion at Frank the barman. 'I didn't say nothin' to no one.'

Frank jumped over the counter and separated them.

'How,' said the doctor to Mary, who was getting more confused herself, 'did he find out these things?'

'Tape recordings,' she said. 'He has been taping everything. He always carries a small digital recorder about with him in his inside pocket. He also has one in his automobile. And he installed a microphone just inside the front garden wall to hear the comments of passers-by.'

'But,' Pat spluttered, 'how did he... find out about... Philadelphia?'

'He had a brilliant idea,' Mary said. 'He sent around with the mailman an automatic mini recorder in a padded yellow envelope addressed to himself. It picked up an immense amount of useful material, though sometimes the quality isn't very good.'

'Useful material?'

'Yes. Didn't you know? He's writing a book about the people here. It's entitled, 'The Language and Imagination of the Irish Peasant'. It will be published next year. He told me he got the idea from his sister, who was once housekeeper to an Irish priest in Surrey. She told him about the quaint way the pastor used to speak and he was so fascinated by the stories she told that he decided to come to Ireland and write a book about it. He was convinced that the best way to get first-hand material was to say nothing himself, act the dummy, and just let the people talk. And he showed me his latest acquisition – a tiny, very sensitive, electronic transmitter he got from France. It picks up all the sounds round about and relays them back to a receiver. You can place it anywhere and you'd hardly notice it, it's so small. Isn't that a brilliant idea!'

A shocked silence reigned in the pub for a time. Though there was some differentiation in the range and intensity of the reactions of the people to Mary's revelations – some were incredulous, some felt betrayed, some felt a bit sheepish, some felt outwitted, some felt humiliated – their feelings gradually started flowing together into one great swell of resentment. So Mr. Dumphries was an English gentleman who called them peasants, spied on them, made a mockery of their language, used them as material, wrote down what they said in a book so that the world could read it and laugh at them.

'That's not right,' muttered Mick Rannigan under his breath, the first ephemeral breeze heralding the approach of a storm.

'Indeed it's not,' said Mrs. Connolly, giving a dirty look to Mary. She had lost again.

'It's not right at all, at all,' said Julia. 'Nobody asked me if I wanted to be in a book!'

'It's the trickery of it that gets me,' said Pat the Post. 'It's downright deceit. In my thirty odd years on the post,' he said, his voice beginning to tremble with the unexpected passion rising within him, 'nobody ever tried to make a fool of me like that. That's what you get for being obliging.' He turned on Mrs. Lavin. 'Will you go out now and try and stick your ould feathery claws in Dumphries' eyes instead of mine?' he asked her. Mrs. Lavin was still too deflated to respond.

'We never liked spies in this country,' said Mick Corcoran, the pig-man, clenching his fist ominously.

'By Christ, we didn't,' added Mick Rannigan, 'nor anyone who didn't respect our priests neither.'

Pints were downed quickly and new rounds ordered. Veins began to stand out on foreheads and bald pates. Voices became deep and raucous or high-pitched and trembling. Eyes flashed, brows knitted, lips tightened. Everybody was saying something, nobody listening. The sounds congealed into one, heavy, solid, dangerous mass of loud, throbbing to talk. Mary couldn't understand it at all.

'But Mr. Dumphries is such a nice, trustworthy man,' she said to Doc Kelly.

Then a shibboleth arose somewhere in the pulsating mass; it hissed first, then crackled and finally spread like wildfire around the lounge: *the tapes! the tapes! the tapes!*

It set the petrol of their pent-up feelings ablaze and suddenly the whole place exploded into action.

'I'm for the Q,' said Mrs. Lavin, now fully recovered, and she strode out the door into the wet night without even putting on her coat.

'After her,' called Pat the Post, and in two minutes flat the lounge was cleared. Mary was swept along in the crowd, leaving her handbag behind on the stool. Lots of the glasses were only half empty. They'd be back soon to finish them.

'God, this is going to be a rough night,' said Sergeant Scally to Frank the barman, 'and me off duty. Well, I suppose I'd better make sure nothing gets out of control. Will you give the P.P. a buzz on your mobile and tell him get out there too. Tell him it's a very urgent sick call! Come on, Doc, we might be needing you!'

Frank quickly phoned the P.P. and was just in time to jump into the sergeant's car as he was pulling away. The only ones left behind in the pub were deaf Bill McCoggan and Sam, the collie. When all were gone, Sam came over to the corner of the red plastic bench where Bill was sitting and curled up at his feet, glad of the peace and quiet again.

The crowd that now took its determined way to Q for Quebec was very different from that which had attended old Andy's funeral only a day before. Some were on foot, some on tractors, some in cars, the majority on bicycles. No procession of mourners these, lamenting the death of a decent neighbour, but an army of roused Celts bent on the protection of their ancient dignity and the defence of their privacy. When Q came into sight, they saw the lights were on. Dumphries working into the night on his perfidious book! He should not escape them. Instinctively they formed a circle around the house, drawing closer and closer.

'Dumphries, come out!' roared Corcoran the pigman, when he got within shouting distance.

No reply.

'You go in and get him,' Mrs. Connolly said to Pat.

'Let Molly Lavin go in first,' said Pat, 'she has the biggest bone to pick with him.'

'No, I'll go in, if I may,' said a voice out of the crowd.

It was Mary. They moved back to make way for her, feeling that under the circumstances she was perhaps best suited for this dramatic role. Mary walked up to the front door, rang the bell and waited. Nothing happened.

'Try the handle,' Julia suggested.

Mary did so, and the unlocked door opened. She went inside. She came out again in a few seconds, stood in the doorway and shrugged her shoulders.

'Nobody here! He's gone!'

They started crowding into the little cottage, that was

the shop. There was a half-empty cup of warm tea on the table, beside it two buttered cream-crackers, the leather-bound notebook with the white pen, and the French book. The grey spotted tie was hanging loosely from a peg on the wall and the jacket of his grey tweed suit was thrown untidily across a chair. The budgie in his covered cage near the window gave a little gurgle and a weak, sleepy chirp and continued with his dreams. The TV was on, but the sound had been switched off. They started to search everywhere. Mick the Pig went into the spotless bedroom and pulled everything apart in his desperate attempt to find the tapes. Mrs. Lavin tried the pantry, Mrs. Connolly the fridge, Martin O'Grady the toilet – which he wanted to use anyway. All to no avail.

'But do we not require a search warrant for this?' asked Mary, her highly-developed sense of civic propriety prompting her to protest. Sergeant Scally, feeling himself indirectly addressed, slipped quietly outside to check when Mick Rannigan suggested the tapes might be in Dumphries' car. But the blue Ford was gone. In the dark he tripped over the flex in the garden and twisted his ankle.

'It seems,' said Doc Kelly, giving expression at last to what they had all begun to realise anyway, 'he knew we were coming, so he skedaddled.'

'And left not a track behind,' quipped Mrs. Connolly.

'But how did he know we were coming?' queried Mary, now totally mesmerized by the proceedings.

'He must have got a tip-off,' Frank the barman said.

Just then a long, painful whine was heard all about the kitchen, followed by a bang and silence. Julia had discovered the receiver under the grey tweed jacket thrown across the chair.

* * *

Bill McCoggan took another nip of his Jameson's.

'Come here, lad, come here,' he said, 'that's enough.'

Sam returned and coiled himself closely around Bill's feet again, shivering and whimpering. He shook his head violently every now and then, as if trying to get something out of his ears. He put his long, pointed snout between his front paws, fixing his guilty eyes, not on the blue leather handbag he had pulled off the stool and torn to bits, nor on the lipstick, the paper handkerchiefs, the letters or the photographs now scattered about on the wet floor of the pub, but on the small black gadget he had viciously mauled and mutilated beyond all recognition because it had been so hurtful to his ears. He was afraid it might start again.

'I don't understand you,' Bill said to Sam, 'you're normally such a quiet, peace-loving dog. I never saw you do a thing like that before. I hope there won't be any trouble when they get back from the hunt. You never know. People are funny, lad. Now can you tell me, Sam, why all of a sudden they had to go off into the night chasing wolves and pheasants? It's not the time of the year for pheasants!'

Sam just lay there, shivering.

DIRTY DAN

Referring to the general lack of knowledge on the part of
people from the city with regard to the things of nature –
trees, flowers, birds – Rober Lynd once wrote: "It is
impossible to take a walk in the country with an average
townsman … without being amazed at the vast continent
of his ignorance." He goes on to say that such ignorance
"is not confined to cuckoos". It extends indeed, one might
contend, to the customs of the country, the lives of country
people, the manners, methods and modes of thought of
country-dwellers at large. You will often hear the man or
woman from the city confess that they could not imagine
themselves exchanging the conveniences of public transport, entertainment centres, medical, social, cultural and
educational infrastructures, for the drab, boring existence
of a peasant community where everybody knows everybody else, and everybody else's business, where nothing
ever changes much, where the only exciting event is a
wedding or a funeral, where interests are limited to cows,
cars and children, and where the GAA provides the main
source of emotional intensity after the honeymoon. The
countryman chuckles to himself when he hears such
confessions. He knows of a different set of references, of
invisible webs of relationships, of unspoken convictions
and myth-making occurrences, of highly-complicated
processes and subtle undertows that permeate everyday
life on the land and from time to time throw up onto its
surface the very memorable occasion, the unsurpassable
achievement, the legendary character, the immortal hero.

The Bold Thady Quill of my home place in the west of Ireland was Dan Dalton, Dan, the anti-hero, Dirty Dan.

Everybody called him Dirty Dan. Our parish consisted at the time of 350 parishioners, who lived in 50 houses, an average of exactly 7 persons per house. And out of those 350 parishioners, 349 called him Dirty Dan. His neighbours called him Dirty Dan, the doctor called him Dirty Dan, the P.P. called him Dirty Dan, Martin the Post brought him letters addressed Dirty Dan. Whenever his name came up in the pub or around the card-table in the evening, he was never referred to as Dan Dalton but simply as Dirty Dan. There were some who didn't even know his real name. But once when I asked my mother if Dominic Dalton, my pal at school, was Dirty Dan's son, she scolded me for using the nickname because, she said, it wasn't a nice thing to call people names. 'Watch your language!' was a warning she was always giving me. My mother was the only one in the parish, I believe, who never called anybody names. To her everybody was simply 'good'. (She herself was nicknamed Typing Tess because she had been a secretary in America and when she came back home she brought with her her old Hammond typewriter which she kept under a grey plastic cover in the corner of the kitchen. Nobody ever saw her use it.)

Our parish was a close-knit, traditional, Christian community, whose forebears had been nature-worshipping, pagan Celts. The people worked the land, there were few blow-ins, everybody, indeed, knew everybody else. Women when they got married took their husband's name, no babies were ever born out of wedlock, children were seen as a blessing, and down the generations the eldest sons bore their father's name and inherited the farms. The daughters were called after their mothers or aunts. One result of this was that a number of individuals often had the same name. We had, for instance, four Mick Flanagans, six

Pat Costelloes, two Johnny Burkes, four Martin Regans and, on the female side, three Bea Freemans, three Rosaleen O'Briens, two Imelda Kennys, to mention but a few of the overlaps. So for purposes of identification and ready reference there inevitably arose the necessity of such nicknames as 'Hairy Mick' and 'Pat-the-Liar' and 'Mary Grandy'. To distinguish families rather than individuals of the same name, our parishioners – a druid race that loved simple numbers, clear lines, subtle thoughts and mysteries, but abhorred confusion of any kind – made use of plain but often inexplicable epithets: the 'hawk' Gradys were not the 'crow' Gradys, the 'bishop' Mangans were not to be confused with the 'bog' Mangans, the 'piper' Crawleys were of a completely different line to the 'clapper' Crawleys, and the 'cuth' Kennys were no relations whatsoever of the 'driney' Kennys.

Some individuals earned their nomenclature on the basis of nature's frolics. Both the 'Damstalk' and the 'Gander' were, in my childhood, middle-aged ladies of ungainly step, more than average height, unmarried and ungraceful. 'Mooney' Deignan had a big, round face. An ethical flaw resulted in the tight-fisted shopkeeper becoming the 'Jew'. Nature in prodigal mood produced 'Solomon', the wise father of four girls and a boy, whose advice was sought by other men when their daughters began staying out late at night, or when, despite the repeated attentions of the bull, a cow still remained infertile. 'Gerry the Gab' was a kind of parochial news agent on a bicycle, with a natural talent for collecting, embellishing and re-telling stories from one end of the parish to the other. Then there were those who owed their nicknames to their occupation, like 'Boxer' Coffey, who once, it was said, fought bare-fisted for the title of World Heavyweight Champion against none other than John. L. Sullivan. 'The Doc', of course, was reserved for the local GP, but 'Doc O'Brien' was a farmer's son who, after studying medicine at Galway University for five years, decided to return home and join the local ceilidh band as a drummer. And there were others again whose nickname derived merely from an unusual historical circumstance. Such was the case with 'Butts' McDermot, whose grandfather had been short taken during Mass because he had breakfasted on a herring that had gone off and who had just made it out the side-door of the church before nature took its inevitable course. In the case of Tommy Flaherty a combination of occupation, physical appearance and circumstance conspired to produce the inevitable nickname. Tommy was small and stocky, had waves of jet black hair, a very sallow complexion, and eyes that were almost black. He worked hard, bringing home the wind-dried turf with his rickety tractor and trailer for half the parish. Rattling up the road on his smoky diesel one Saturday evening in August, coated with the dust and dirt of twenty bogs, he was met by Pat-the-Liar who was on his way to Connolly's, the butcher's, to get a pound of the fresh sirloin steak advertised as 'lion chops' in the midge-infested window. 'I just met Flaherty on his tractor and do you know I thought he was a nigger first,' he confided to Mrs. Connolly. The name stuck, and even his three blonde daughters were known as the 'Nigger' Flaherty girls till marriage eventually put paid to the incongruity.

But while many families and most individuals were identified by names other than, or supplementary to, those entered in the Baptismal registry, it would be a mistake to consider the surrogate appellations as being all on the same level and of equal value, though most had the sole function of facilitating identification. You could classify them into three groups.

There were the nicknames which were universally used in the parish – used even by the nicknamed themselves –

and which were non-offensive, generations old, purely functional and self-explanatory. A stranger drove into the parish one day, a man down from Dublin to investigate a proposed drainage scheme. He saw a local in wellington boots digging ridges for potatoes near the road. He pulled up, took out a slip of paper, and scrutinizing it through thick spectacles, walked over to the farmer and asked him if he knew where James O'Donnell lived.

'We have three James O'Donnells around here. If it's Spade O'Donnell you're looking for, I'm your man.'

The civil servant said the James O'Donnell he was looking for was from the town land of Augheraboy.

'That'd be Red Jimmy, now,' said Spade, and giving the man exact directions how to get to Augheraboy, he continued his digging.

'Would you be Red Jimmy O'Donnell?' ventured the near-sighted civil servant when he drew up at Jimmy's house.

'Yes, I am,' said Jimmy, 'redder you won't get. You're from the Department, aren't you? I've been expecting you. Pleased to meet you. Come in'

No offence, no embarrassment, a man's instinctive, natural respect for his own genes.

The second group consisted of names of recent coinage, more restricted in use, not necessarily known to everyone in the parish, and either harmless or dangerous if applied directly to the person concerned, according to his mood, his relation to the user, or the presence of bystanders. Solomon's young son was only seven as he sat one summer day picking daisies on a sunny bank by the side of the road. Along came Pat Malone on his squeaking bicycle. 'Hello, Spud,' greeted the innocent child. The timing was perfect. Pat got the full, clear force of both words just as he was passing. Result psychological: Pat exploded at hearing the nickname he so detested. Result visible: Pat, child, daisies and bicycle in a tangle in the ditch. Result audible: thumps, whimpers, a wheezing chest, words like 'bold pup', 'bad bringing up', cursing. Conclusion philosophical: a sense of danger, unlike red hair, is not transferred with the genes. In our parish everyone had to learn – sometimes the hard way – that the rules of the names game were based on very categorical imperatives.

The third group included those nicknames that one dared not use directly to the person or family in question, nor to any blood or marriage relations. You only used these names within the safe confines of your own family, or when talking to a small circle of close friends stood outside the church after Sunday Mass, or in the presence of four or five trusted neighbours squeezed into O'Brien's snug after drawing the pension on Friday. To this day I still don't know if the 'piper' Crawleys knew they were called 'The Pipers', but I never heard the name used by anyone except our family (in whispers, when the door was locked) and the aunts down the road, who knew nobody at all by their right name. Today if I happen to see on TV a band of kilted Scotsmen with their bagpipes parading at a festival, or hear a fife and drum band on the radio playing a selection of marches, a shudder of terror comes rippling along my veins from those far-off days. So deep was my fear of those hooligan Crawleys, who fought outside the dance-hall every Saturday night, sometimes with 6-inch nails in their hands, and once castrated Mick Madigan's boar because Mick wouldn't hand over Mary Mulrennan, home on holidays from Australia, to the oldest Crawley brother (there were five of the thugs) at the 'change partners' dance, that one bitterly cold winter morning many years later that shudder suddenly went through me again as I was desperately trying to get the water flowing in our frozen pipes, and, on another occasion, as I stood looking up at the massive organ pipes in St. Stephen's Cathedral in Vienna.

That Dan Dalton, then, should have a nickname was something perfectly natural, for there were three Dalton families and two Dan Daltons in the parish, and each had to be identified. That he should be called Dirty Dan was, perhaps, perfectly natural, too. But that he should universally be called Dirty Dan – universally, that is, in parochial terms – was not at all natural. Or at least it wasn't quite logical. That everyone (except my mother) repeatedly and unquestioningly used the term when referring to Dan could easily lead the hygienic-minded outsider to the logical conclusion that, except for Dan, our parish consisted solely of clean men and women. Now it cannot be denied we had some paragons of hygiene of either sex living in the community. There was Nurse Corrigan, the parish midwife, who was unanimously accorded the gold medal for cleanliness because she was known to have 10 identical white uniforms, and each Saturday morning exactly five of them hung on the clothes-line in her garden as the Bord-na-mona workers passed to work on their push-bikes at quarter to eight. And there was Mrs. Mahon: at school her disconsolate son envied his pal, Joey Maloney, his dirty shoes and his half-washed face and the luxury of teeth not brushed for weeks. Young Mahon said: 'I wish I had a dirty mother like you.' But Maloney, offended, told when he went home and the Maloneys and the Mahons didn't speak for years. Mrs. Cassidy, too, was a clean woman and Mrs. Rafferty and 10 or 15 more. And some men, perhaps more secretively, were also as clean as could reasonably be expected. Jimmy Gilligan, who lived alone, never let the dishes pile up for more than one meal, and in summer when the lake was warm he went for a daily dip and always took his bar of carbolic soap along with him. What he did in winter

77

remained a moot question. John Regan was called 'Shine' because his shoes were always so well polished. But one wet day a travelling salesman called on John and convinced him of the value of galoshes. The next Sunday it was still raining and John wore the galoshes to Mass. When he took them off in the porch, his shiny patent leather shoes were covered with a layer of moist dust. Embarrassed, John knelt at the very back and kept his feet well pulled in under him all during Mass. In a vibrant parish that loved tradition and clarity and mystery, the slightest change of anybody's wonted position in church on Sunday couldn't go unnoticed and required explanation. John Regan's new position (five seats further back than usual) and unaccustomed posture (he was known to stretch out his left foot around gospel time and his right one just after the consecration) made him more conspicuous for a time than the priest at the altar. Then the shoes were spotted and, a week or so later, another of those anonymous poems from the intellectual underworld, which circulated mysteriously from time to time as occasion arose, had 5 of its 50 lines dedicated to John:

> *John, John, the shine is gone!*
> *Was it the pools and closhes?*
> *Or that clever Dick*
> *With his saleman's tricks*
> *That made you buy galoshes?*

There were, I'm sure, 10 or 15 other men, too, whom you could say were very clean, in their person and in their habits, even if less ostensibly so than the ladies. Now nobody knows for certain who first used the term Dirty Dan, but that it should have originated among this group is a perfectly logical and tenable theory.

However, there was a second group from which the anonymous authorship might have stemmed, though this is less likely. The parish had a large grey majority of either sex whom you could not describe as clean, nor to whom you could in fairness or with accuracy refer to as really dirty. They consisted mainly of down-to-earth people who looked with suspicion on hygiene as such, and who believed that a certain amount of dirt was clean and healthy and, in fact, strengthened the body's resistance to infectious diseases. These were people who wore a clean shirt or blouse on Sunday but saw no need for detergents, who wore good woollen suits or topcoats in winter but cared nothing for launderettes or dry-cleaning. The men wore long-johns by day and slept in them at night. Empiricists by instinct and believers by tradition, they only washed their hands when they were visibly dirty. They believed in a God that was invisible, but not in invisible bacteria. The natural subtlety of their minds taught them to distinguish between dirts. There was bog dirt, for example, which was, in fact, clean and you could even drink bog water. Even soot could be clean, or have cleansing effects. My father was once told that to rub a bit of wet soot on the teeth every day was the best way to make them glow, and for weeks my mother had to put a spoonful on a saucer for him each morning in the bathroom. When we children discovered this we surreptitiously glanced in our father's mouth from time to time but, seeing no change, we gradually began to identify this strange custom with its practitioner and secretly started calling our father 'Soot'. That's the only nickname of whose origin I am absolutely certain.

Then there was dirty dirt. To this category belonged primarily faeces of all kinds, and any man (or woman) who went to collect the pension or do the week-end shopping with cow-dung on his shoes was in great danger of being counted among the dirty – unless special circumstances exonerated him. Old Johnny Conroy was as neat and jaunty a little man as ever milked a cow, but when his wife set sail for England to visit the daughter in Coventry and never returned, his consequent degeneration – unshaven even on Sundays, black finger-nails, drooling tobacco stains on his formerly white shirt – did not qualify him as dirty, in the technical sense, but as unfortunate, and that was a different category altogether.

Now what was natural, but not logical, in Dan Dalton's being universally (except for my mother) and naturally called Dirty Dan was that it seemed so natural to everybody that he should be universally called Dirty Dan. Let me explain.

We had a common saying in our parish that if one man pointed the finger at another and was himself not without blame it was a case of the pot calling the kettle black. The old Parish Priest who, in the days before the liturgical revival, used to quench the candles on the altar with a smart tap of the burse on finishing the last gospel, was known for his valiant efforts to make scripture more intelligible to his flock. He knew that no one knew exactly what a 'mote' in one's own eye really was; even 'beam' was doubtful. But everybody knew what a pot and a kettle were and the sacred text was exegeted accordingly: 'Before you see the kettle in your neighbour's eye, take the pot out of your own,' he said. Now the eternal tug between objectivity and subjectivity, the problem of seeing things straight in the eye, just as they are, came to the surface once more in the case of Dirty Dan in a new variation. It was natural that a clean man should see a dirty man as dirty; it was natural, if reprehensible, that a half-clean or fully dirty man, should, or could, see a dirty man as dirty and not see himself as half-dirty or dirty. But it was not logical that all the half-dirties, and all the cleanies, should think it natural that even the dirties should naturally call Dan Dirty Dan. And perhaps strangest of all was the fact that when it was observed that my mother never used the term Dirty Dan at all, she was latently accused of unnaturally calling the kettle white by implication. But that's another matter. It remained a quirk in the common psyche of our parishioners that they unanimously used the term when talking of Dan and were universally thought moteless in doing so.

It was certainly natural, in any case, to call Dan Dalton Dirty Dan. For he was really dirty, very very dirty. Dan, who never got married and lived alone, died of dirt. His finger-nails decayed and fell off. He couldn't close his eye-lids for the dirt caked in the corners, so he slept with open eyes. His nose kept running day and night and the sneezes he sprayed over the table formed a myriad of microscopic drops that were held together by dust and gradually formed a depository of decomposed flies. His one hanky was black and tattered. His bushy, grey beard was heavy with the weight of mildewed food remnants lodged there. When they chiselled off his boots after his demise, a yellow shred of the Roscommon Herald that Dan had put inside his only pair of socks five years earlier to try and keep his feet warm, fell out. His last breakfast in his ramshackle cottage he shared with three old mice. Originally there had been five, but two had died the previous evening after Dan put a slice of unprecedented cheddar cheese on his plate. For months he had survived on tea and cottage cheese and all six of them – Dan and the five mice – had grown accustomed to the diet. But whereas Dan was getting thinner and thinner, the mice were getting fatter and fatter. Then the shopkeeper ran out of cottage cheese and Dan had to try the cheddar. That evening all six stuffed themselves cheddar full. The anonymous poet's pen recorded a parody:

Five fat mice,
See how they thrive!
They all have a liking for Danny's cheese:
But it's Cheddar, not Cottage, now, if you please!
Be careful, dear Dan, or you'll catch a disease
From those five fat mice.

However, the two mice with the weaker constitutions just dragged themselves away from Dan's plate and dropped dead simultaneously of heart failure over the side of the table. When the three surviving mice crept to breakfast the next morning over the carcasses of their cheese-killed comrades, they arrived at Dan's plate only to find it empty except for a few drops of spittle, blood and dirt which had emanated from his open mouth on his last, expiring breath. He was discovered two days later by Martin The Post, who immediately called the priest. Dan was not laid out in the usual way but simply wrapped up as he was in a black cloth, put in a coffin and brought to the church. Next day they buried him in the cemetery after the funeral Mass, and on the request of distant relatives, and by way of exception, and without wishing to be seen as in any way setting a precedent, whereas they were otherwise totally committed to putting out fires, the fire brigade moved out to the cottage, set it ablaze and burned it to the ground.

My mother didn't attend Dan's funeral. That morning I had black rims around my eyes, it seems, so she kept me at home from school and was looking after me. She gave me a spoonful of the dreaded senna pods, her cure for all ailments, and in those days of behind-the-ditch toilets and grass toilet paper the purgative, in addition to its awful taste, made life for a schoolboy very awkward. 'It might give you the runs, son,' she said, 'but you'll see: in two or three days you'll be right as rain and back to school.' If ever there was a Hobson's choice!

I was crouched behind the ditch on my fifth run, with my mother nearby cutting nettles for the turkeys and getting her bare arms all stung, when who should come cycling slowly along the road but Gerry The Gab on his way home from the funeral, and the pub. My mother spotted him, and being anxious, as ever, to hear the latest news, called out to him as he was passing:

'How did the funeral go, Gerry?'

Gerry gladly dismounted, and I crouched lower and lower, mortified in case he might see me.

'A small enough crowd,' he said, leaning across the handlebars and obviously in no hurry. 'I think a lot of people were afraid to go. You never could tell, Teresa, what you might pick up. Dan, as you know, was a bit shy of the soap and the water.'

'I'm sure he's in heaven, anyway,' said my mother.

'No doubt he is,' said Gerry, 'sure he never did no hurt to man nor mouse. Did you hear what the fire brigade done?'

'No. What?'

'Arra, they razed his little cottage to the ground. Look, it's still smouldering!'

Off in the distance black clouds of smoke were still billowing into the sky. Forgetting myself, I stood up to have a look, too.

'Why isn't the ladeen at school?' asked Gerry, when he saw me.

I froze with embarrassment, not even able to duck down again. I knew I had dirtied my pants. But my tactful mother easily turned Gerry's attention away from my predicament.

'Do you know what, Gerry,' she said, 'you come around this evening when my husband is back, I'll put the kettle on, we'll have a game of 25 and you can tell us all about it in detail. I have to boil these nettles now for the turkeys or they'll gobble me up.'

'Right!' said Gerry, and off he went – to my immense relief.

Gerry returned that evening for the game of cards and the story-telling. I heard him leave around ten o'clock, long after I had gone to bed. A little later my mother came upstairs and tiptoed to my bedside and kissed my hot forehead. Then she went back down the stairs.

Three days later I was, indeed, as right as rain again and back at school. When we got out to play, Jamie Creaton, Solomon's son, said to me:

'Did you hear the poem about Dirty Dan?'

'No,' I said.

'Well, listen. It has 25 verses. I might not be able to say them all.'

He began reciting.

You're gone, good Dan, and may you rest in peace.
You never did no hurt to man nor mouse.
Your tastes were simple, and the gentle beasts
Found food and comfort in your humble house.

It's sad to see your cottage now a-smouldering
And lazy cats enjoying roasted mouse.
In the cold clay your body now is mouldering
While firemen's flames have razed your little house.

So what, if you were shy of soap and water!
So what, if you survived on cheese and tea!
Not every man has got a wife or daughter
To cook his meals and wash his handkerchief.

'Wait,' I said, interrupting Jamie, 'I think I have heard bits of that somewhere before!'

The bell rang for the end of play.

'I'll say the rest for you after school,' Jamie promised.

When I got home that evening I said to my mother:

'There's a new poem out about Dirty Dan. It goes ...'

'How often,' she interrupted, 'must I tell you not to be calling people names. Here, eat your dinner and then go and do your homework.'

It was then I noticed the grey plastic cover was off the typewriter in the corner and a sheet of paper was in the carriage.

FALSE FRIENDS

Pat and Mick were, as they say, two brothers. They had the same birthday, September 1st, but Pat was one year older than Mick. Cut out of their grandfather on their mother's side, they both had dark hair and blue eyes. Like two peas in a pod, the neighbours said. Twelve years long, Pat was taller than his brother, but then Mick drew level. After that, any difference in height was due to variations in their hair style. At one stage, when he was away in college, Pat shaved every rib of hair off his head, it being mod at the time, while Mick, who never went to boarding school, let his thick and wavy hair grow like the rest of the country boys. For a while that made Mick look taller than Pat, but he wasn't. They were exactly the same height. Most people who didn't know the Quinn family well took the two boys for twins. Weak-sighted Mrs. Noone, too old to ride her bicycle now, and too mean to take the bus, often walked by their house on her way into the village to collect the pension when the boys were out playing in the front garden. If it was Pat she saw first she'd invariably say, 'Hello, Mickeen, I thought first it was Pat.' If it was Mick she saw, she'd say, 'Hello Pateen, I thought first it was Mick.' She always got it wrong.

Pat and Mick lived with their father and mother in a plain, two-storey house on a fairly large farm by West of Ireland standards. They were not poor and they were not rich. They had no television, because Mrs. Quinn wanted to protect her boys from evil influences. They had no telephone, because Mr. Quinn feared the consequences, especially financial, of encouraging that particular channel of communication in his house. The strong Catholic farmer owned a big Massey Ferguson, bulled his own cows, but was prepared, without further ado, to step down on that third great manifestation of success among the agricultural community in Ireland, a son in Maynooth. Now that that ecclesiastical establishment was no longer the preserve of clerical students but was open to lay boys, and, as a local wit observed, to lay girls, too, it had lost a lot of its prestige value in his eyes. He didn't mind whether Pat or Mick went to Maynooth or not, but on no account would he accept both going there! In any case, the problem never arose, for neither son showed the slightest sign of a vocation.

Mrs. Quinn helped her husband with light work about the farm. She fed the chickens, weeded the vegetable patch (using rubber gloves), scoured the milk cans for the creamery, cut the seed potatoes into splits for sowing in spring (making sure there was an eye in each split), and made good healthy stews for her 'three men' when the weather was cold. She was also fond of entertaining friends, writing letters to relatives in America, reading detective novels and cookery books, and doing Irish step-dancing. She went to the hairdresser's every Friday, to Mass every Sunday, and to the Dublin Horse Show every August, always taking advantage of the occasion to visit Andrew in Harold's Cross. She was proud of her brother and the very good job he had in the civil service. Whenever she was in the capital she went to the dogs with him at the local greyhound racing track, for she loved dogs. 'Man's best friend,' she would say, placing a little wager on dog no.1. She always put her money on the dog in trap 1, and she usually came out winners.

Her husband went to the pub on Saturdays, Mass on Sundays, and football matches on Sunday afternoons.

Mr. and Mrs Quinn were both proud of their two sons and had good, if not every, reason to be so. The boys hardly every quarrelled with each other, did well at school, helped out on the farm whenever they had to without complaining, and never got into trouble much. There was, of course, the Sunday when their father had gone to see the Roscommon vs. Mayo game and Pat and Mick decided to go fishing. Instead of walking the mile or so to the lake as usual, they took out the big Massey Ferguson and made their daredevil way across the fields, through gaps and fences, over drains and ditches, down to the lakeside, followed by faithful Jacko, barking with delight. The ground looked solid enough, but the treacherous, dried surface only concealed the swampland beneath. They drove too near the edge of the water and suddenly, despite the 300 horse power, the four-wheel traction and the massive double tyres, the tractor began to subside in the mud. They jumped off and ran back in panic to tell their mother. She raised the alarm, and soon the County Council lorry with the mounted crane arrived on the scene. But when they tried to lift the tractor out, the back wheels of the lorry sank in the mud, too, and the crane toppled into the water. So they had to open the sluices at the end of the lake and lower the water level in order to salvage the machinery. Returning from the football match hours later, Mr. Quinn couldn't believe his eyes when he saw the lake half gone and his own fine tractor submerged in the mud. A rescue party was organized and a fleet of local tractors using pulleys and steel ropes finally got the lorry, the crane and the Massey Ferguson back on dry land again. As punishment, Mr. Quinn suspended the boys' pocket money for a time (the rescue operation had proved very costly). Mrs. Quinn said it was not the boys' fault, and blamed her husband for leaving the keys in the ignition. For a long time the topic of fishing was avoided in the Quinn family.

Pat was twelve and Mick was eleven when the tractor incident occurred.

Or there was the time, five years before that, on 1st April, when Pat got Mick to write a letter of farewell to their parents, as an April Fool's trick. They took a leaf out of their Mammy's writing pad, and one of her airmail envelopes, and after dinner, instead of going out to play as usual, crept quietly to their room upstairs to write the letter. It read, in Mick's uncertain letters:

Dear mammy and daddy, I'm leevin for ever. Gud by. Your fond son, Mick.

They both thought it was very, very funny They slipped it under Mick's pillow, and when nobody was looking went outside. Mick hid behind the hayshed, and Pat whispered in Jacko's ear not to let on. Jacko was their best friend, they could rely on him. Around 6 o'clock Mrs. Quinn called her husband and the two boys in to tea. Pat sat opposite his father at the table but couldn't look him in the eyes for fear of bursting out laughing. After a while his mammy said:

'Where's Michael?'

Pat bit his lip and said nothing.

'Will you go out and tell him his tea's ready.'

Pat dashed out, but was back in half a minute.

'No sight of him anywhere!'

'Maybe he's upstairs,' said Mr. Quinn. 'Go up and see.'

Again Pat was back in a shot.

No he isn't. But look, I found this under his pillow.'

'That was very quick!' said his father.

Pat gave the envelope to his mammy, keeping his eyes down as she read the letter. But he saw that her hand was trembling a little as she handed it to her husband.

'Now what might this mean?' said Mr. Quinn, looking suspiciously at his son. 'Do you know anything about it?'

'No,' lied Pat. But it wasn't really a lie, it was only April

Fool's.

'I'm going for the police,' announced Mrs. Quinn, beginning to panic as some vague sequence from a frightening detective story went racing across her mind.

'Nonsense,' said her husband, 'he must be around somewhere. Come on, Pat, let's look for him.'

He left the table and went outside, Pat following at his heels and Jacko bringing up the rear. But it was too much for Mrs. Quinn. She mounted her bicycle and rode to the police station. She was taking no risks. Ten minutes later two uniformed gardai arrived back on the farm with Mrs. Quinn in the back of the blue squad car. First they looked for Mick in the house and then went out to join Mr. Quinn and Pat in the search around the yard and the outhouses. The longer the search went on, the more distraught Mrs. Quinn was becoming. Then suddenly Jacko started barking like mad and wagging his tail. Pat gave him a kick and told him be quiet, but the dog would not be put off the scent. He nearly wagged the tail off himself with excitement as he got closer to the hayshed, finally betraying Mick's hideout. Mick came running out from behind the shed.

'April Fool' he screeched in delight. His glee knew no bounds, so well had the trick worked. They really thought he had gone and were out searching for him. And if Jacko hadn't given him away, they would still be looking for him. Pat tried to give Jacko another leather injection, but this time the clever sheepdog saw the boot coming and deftly placed himself out of range, taking refuge behind Mrs. Quinn's legs. Then Mick noticed the two gardai.

'What are they doing here?' he asked Pat.

'Looking for you,' said Pat.

'Here I am,' said Mick.

The policemen looked at Mrs. Quinn and then at her husband. Shaking their heads in unison, they began their discreet withdrawal from the farmyard.

'Boys will be boys,' said one of them, as they got into the squad car and drove away.

Mick got a big hug from his mother.

'It's all your fault,' said Mr. Quinn to his wife, 'leaving your writing pad and envelopes hanging around like that.'

Then he gave Mick a sharp box on the ear and sent him upstairs to bed, without any supper. Pat's role in the kidology remained undiscovered by his parents, but when he got into bed beside his brother two hours later, Mick was still awake, and sulking.

'It was your stupid idea!' he said. 'Take that, Pat!'

He tried to kick his brother under the sheets.

'Don't kick, Mick!' said Pat.

After a second's pause, they both started laughing at what they had said. They repeated it.

'Take that, Pat!'

'Don't kick, Mick!'

They laughed again. And then again. And then again once more. And now they couldn't stop. A short pause to take breath, and then off into the giggles again. That went on for half an hour until they finally fell asleep, exhausted from laughing.

That was the beginning of a words game that the two brothers were to play over and over again in the years to come. They developed it and they delighted in it. They competed with each other for rhymes, composed little poems, and sometimes just put delightful nonsense-words together that wouldn't have made sense to anybody else.

Well brought up, well behaved, well liked by the neighbours, the two Quinn boys were undoubtedly a credit to their parents. Occasionally their father felt a little disappointed that neither son had the slightest interest in Gaelic football, or any other kind of sport for that matter. They liked fishing, of course, but that was more a pastime than a sport and didn't call for very much physical exertion. However, he never gave expression to his feelings on that point. There were times, too, when their mother felt a little disappointed that neither of them was a girl, but whenever such thoughts came into her mind she immediately put them aside as being 'uncomely emotions' (a nice phrase she had read somewhere) and unworthy of a Christian mother. And she never gave expression to her feelings on that point to anybody, least of all to her husband. She didn't really formulate them for herself.

Another point where the Quinn boys didn't quite come up to the expectations of their parents was the matter of Irish songs and dancing and music. When they were nine (eight) they were sent to take lessons in Irish step-dancing, but after three weeks of tough going, fair-minded Miss Darcy sent a discreet note to their parents telling them that the boys, though not altogether lacking in talent, didn't seem terribly interested in her work and maybe it might be wiser, and less expensive, if they concentrated on some other branch of traditional Irish culture. (Pat: 'Can't dance!' Mick: 'Got our chance!')

Mr. Quinn was very proud of everything Irish, though his double-row, button-key accordion in C was a Hohner. 'German products are the most reliable,' was his defence whenever he was challenged on the point. On his Hohner he would often play Irish melodies and dance-music for hours on end during the long winter evenings when it got dark around five and there wasn't any work to do outside after the cows and calves had been fed and the chickens locked up for the night. Sometimes the endless jigs and reels and hornpipes were too much even for Mrs. Quinn and gave her a 'reeling' headache (her favourite quip), and she would ask him to stop 'rasping' because Patrick and Michael upstairs couldn't concentrate on their homework. But most of the time the boys had the radio on in any case, or were listening to their favourite Bob Dylan and Joan

Baez cassettes. Once a year, on or around St. Patrick's Day, the Quinns invited all the local farmers to a 'do' in their house. Then sturdy legs in hob-nailed boots would hammer out half-sets and highland flings and sieges of Ennis on the hard, stone floor of the spacious kitchen, with Mr. Quinn on his Hohner doing great honour to the national saint, supported by Tim Mulcahy on the tin whistle and Johnny Higgins on the fiddle. On these occasions the 'twins' couldn't escape upstairs because there were little chores they had to do, like passing around the chicken sandwiches to the guests and filling up empty stout glasses from the 10-gallon barrel of Guinness. Mr. Quinn had a nice singing voice, and when the breathless dancers took time out for refreshments, either Mulcahy or Higgins would call for silence and a song, giving their host the required opportunity. Then Mr. Quinn would stand up by the range, without having to be asked twice, and sing his favourite ballad, *The Old Bog Road*. The inevitable encore was always *Galway Bay*. This gradually became an embarrassment for Mick and Pat, and by the time they were finishing primary school they could hardly bear any more to hear,

> *My feet are here on Broadway*
> *This blessed Christmas morn,*
> *And, oh, the ache that's in them*
> *For the place where I was born!*

But it was always the same on St. Patrick's day and they couldn't escape. Making the best of it, when they got to bed they would sing the parody they had once heard on the radio, Pat taking the first and third lines, Mick the second and fourth, and so on:

> Pat: *My feet are here, they're broad ones*
> Mick: *This blessed Christmas morn,*
> Pat: *But, oh, the ache that's in them*
> Mick: *From ingrown nails and corns.*

The boys had nice singing voices, too, but not for Irish songs.

The first time the 'twins' were separated was when Pat finished primary school. Being the elder of the two and destined by tradition to inherit the farm, he went away, or more precisely was sent away, to an agricultural college. In the modern world it was necessary for a young farmer to know all about biological farming, slurry disposal, organic and inorganic fertilisers, genetic engineering, farm management and even holidays on the farm. So one morning in September, shortly after his thirteenth birthday, Pat found himself on the train to Dublin, accompanied by his mother. There was sadness in his blue eyes because all the time the diesel was taking him relentlessly away from his father and the farm and the uncaught fish in the lake and Jacko. Worst of all, it was taking him away from Mick. Pat hated the train. When they got to the capital, it was at least a bus that would take them out to Gormanstown where the agricultural college was. Mrs. Quinn tried to cheer her son up by telling him that he would make lots of new friends in the boarding school, and that it was only a few short weeks till the Christmas holidays, and that it was very important for a farmer today to be well educated if he wanted to succeed. But at heart Pat did not care a lot for farm work and he would have much preferred to go to an ordinary college like Nathy's, where most of his school friends went. He could come home every evening and help a bit on the farm if he had to, and do his homework, and listen to his cassettes, and rhyme the evening to a close with Mick beside him in the twin bed. But if his parents wanted him to go away to an agricultural college, there wasn't much he could do about it.

The first letter dutiful Pat wrote from Gormanstown was to his mammy and daddy. It was short: there were 28 boys in his class, the bed was hard, the food was good, he missed them, and Mick, and Jacko, and he was already looking forward to Christmas. The next day another, longer, letter arrived for Mick. Pat told him a lot about the boys in the college: some were very big and rough, some he couldn't understand, some were gone mad on Gaelic football. In his class there were three boys from other countries with strange names: Louis from France, Miguel from Spain and Karl from Austria. Whereas Louis and Miguel were small and had sallow skin, Karl was the same height and complexion as Pat. He himself was the only one from the west of Ireland. The teachers were very friendly. Classes hadn't started yet. He would write soon again. He ended: 'Cheerio. I have to go. The bell is ringing, the Franciscans are singing! Your fondest brother (you have no other!), Pat.'

Throughout his first year as a boarder in Gormanstown, Pat wrote regularly to Mick, and Mick usually replied within a week or two. When Pat was home for the Christmas and Easter holidays they spent many hours together walking over the fields and around the lake, mostly with Pat telling stories about the college, and the boys there, and the teachers. Some subjects he liked very much, like biology and maths, and some he found very boring, like history and geography. But the ones that interested him least of all were those that were directly connected with agriculture: crop rotation, cross-breeding, fertilization, organic farming, BSE, foot-and-mouth, pasture planning and so on. He was surprised that the foreign boys knew so much about Ireland. Karl from Austria had a little album with lots of cuttings he had collected from newspapers and magazines, and he could tell Pat many things about the Celts in Austria, and Virgil, the Irish saint who built the cathedral in Salzburg, and Irish soldiers who fought in the army of Maria Theresa. Louis from France filled him in on General Lambert who landed in Kilalla in 1798 to help the Irish beat the British, and on the Irish soldiers who fought in Napoleon's army: Avenue McMahon in Paris, for instance, was named after an Irish general. And the Spanish boy, Miguel, knew all about the Spanish ships that landed in Kinsale in 1601 to help Hugh O'Neill: back home he had seen a wonderful documentary about it on TV. Pat often felt embarrassed that he knew very little about France or Spain or Austria. He would love to visit those countries one day and learn more.

'So you see,' Mick said, 'we badly need a television set. Tell mammy about the documentary and she might agree to one at last.'

'Not a bad idea,' said Pat. 'Then I'll be able to tell the Flyers something about their countries, too.'

'Who are the Flyers?' asked Mick.

'Oh, that's what we call Karl, Louis and Miguel: KLM. Got it?

'NOPe', said Mick, 'but I'm QRiouS!'

The two brothers got on so well together.

Mick was even less fond of farm work than Pat and, being the younger of the two, he was glad that he was not subject to the same inheritance pressure as his brother. When he told his parents he would like to go to the local college after primary, they had no objections whatsoever. In fact his father immediately bought him a 21-speed Kettler mountain bike (reliable German product) to take him on the 3-kilometre trip to the town. As the road, however, was perfectly level and only rose slightly at the approach to the big, high gates of the college, 19 of the 21 gears were completely superfluous.

At the age of 13, then, Mick started off as a day-boy in Nathy's College, and he liked it from the word go. He came home every afternoon at 3.30 and spent a lot of time at his books, especially Latin. He was very fond of Latin. At one stage the President of the College suggested to him that he might think of studying for the priesthood. Mick didn't say no, but inwardly it was the last thing on his mind. He didn't want to spend his life as a parish priest among farmers who had never crossed the Shannon. Nor did he intend to spend his life on the farm in Kiltimore, either. Influenced, perhaps, by Pat's stories, what Mick desired most of all was to travel. All the romantic place-names he saw in Pat's atlas – Andalusia, Montenegro, Fontainebleau, Vienna, Alicante, San Sebastian – fascinated him. One day Pat told him about a special project that everybody had had to do for the farm management class. Karl from Austria had chosen the theme of farm holidays. Part of his presentation was a video he showed of his native country. Pat marvelled at the large, old farmhouses with the small windows, walls of reddish stone, solid wooden balconies and steep roofs; the sheds for the animals attached to the farmhouses; the incredible slant of the pasture slopes of the Alpine foothills, that must be terribly dangerous for tractors and cows. And always in the background the spiky snow-covered mountain peaks going up and down like graphs in mathematics. When the teacher asked Karl if avalanches ever came down those mountains, he remained strangely silent. Mick loved these stories.

Mick: *It must be a marvellous country ...*
Pat: *It must indeed ...*
Mick: *And I'm beginning to wonder ...*
Pat: *It's coming, I can see it ...*
Mick: *If you or I might one day ...*
Pat: *Have the luck to set our feet ...*
Mick: *On those lovely Alpine uplands ...*
Pat: *Or the snowy mountain peaks.*

Long before his final year in secondary school Mick had made up his mind: when he had done his Leaving Cert, he would go abroad and see the world.

After five years Pat finished his secondary education in Gormanstown. The last day before the Leaving Cert class broke up, all his classmates exchanged addresses and promised they would write to each other and keep in touch. Glad, in one way, to be back on the tractor in Kiltimore and home once more from the agricultural college he had grown in the end to detest, Pat started letting his hair grow again while waiting for the Leaving Cert results to come out. He had no intention of keeping up contact with any of his schoolmates. The ones he got on best with, the Flyers, had gone back to their respective countries.

That summer was a pleasant one for the Quinn family. The sun shone from the end of May through to September, and there was very little rain. The crops were good, the cattle thrived, the boys were cooperative. Only, Mr. Quinn was not too willing to accept Pat's new ideas about fertilisers and crop rotation. And the joy of Mrs. Quinn's visit to the Horse Show in Dublin was dampened by only one little stroke of bad luck: not once in a whole evening's racing did the dog in trap 1 win.

'Your best friends sometimes let you down!' Andrew teased.

The results of the Leaving came out in August. They were not brilliant as far as Pat was concerned, but at least he had passed all subjects. His mother was disappointed that he had not got enough points to go to university, but Mr. Quinn, without expressing his feelings openly, was very satisfied that his son would from now on be devoting all his time to the farm that he was one day to inherit. For other reasons Pat himself found the results very accept-able. It was Mr. Quinn who finally convinced his wife that it would be a nice reward for Pat, and useful for Mick, too, if they invested in a television set. Despite its negative effects, television was also educational and would surely be a great advantage for their sons and help them in keeping up-to-date with the latest developments in politics and science. In the back of his mind he was also thinking of the football matches on TV and the Ceoltas Ceoiltoiri Eireann programmes. Mrs. Quinn's efforts to convince her husband that the telephone was an equally important investment were less successful.

In September Mick started his last year at St. Nathy's. Every evening when he came home he spent many hours in his room at his books, with music playing in the background. Somehow it helped him to concentrate. Pat, in order not to distract him, often sat on the couch in the living-room watching TV. Since they got the television set, the brothers' taste in music had changed dramatically. One reason was an extraordinary discovery Pat had made. He chanced to zap in one evening on an ITVl documentary on Robbie Williams. To his utter astonishment, he saw that the boy band of which that famous singer was originally a member was called Take That.

'Well, that takes the biscuit,' said Mick, when Pat told him.

'Maybe they stole the title from us!'

'Very true. Let's sue!'

But instead of suing, they took the very next opportunity to invest their pocket money in *Life Thru A Lens* and *I've Been Expecting You*, and now *Blowin' in the Wind* and *In the Quiet Morning* and all those other lyrics that were their musical friends for so many years, had to give way to *South Of The Border* and *Old Before I Die* and *Angels*. Baez and Dylon were dethroned to make way for Take That, and Boyzone, and Westlife, and New Kids On The Block, and Robbie Williams. This was the music now that provided background inspiration for Pat as he wrestled with Homer's Iliad and Cicero's speeches and the history of Europe and the convolutions of commercial geography. When Mrs. Quinn downstairs heard the music, she'd throw her eyes up to heaven and direct a semi-rhetorical question at her husband: 'Where is this all going to end?' His only comment was: 'Well, it's not my kind of music.'

Shortly before Christmas Pat received an unexpected postcard from Karl in Vienna. It showed a portrait of a very upright Johann Strauss, with a big moustache and waves of thick hair, playing the violin. The postcard read:

> *Hello Pat! I wish you a merry Christmas and a happy New Year. I miss Irland very much. I now study at Vienna. My main subject is forestry, but I also visit English language classes. I don't want to forget my English. I do a special project: I collect False Friends, like 'fast' and 'civil servants'. Perhaps you can help me get a few more. Write to me sometimes – hope you still have my adress. Auf wiedersehen, my friend.*
> *Karl.*

'What do you think of that?' said Pat to Mick, handing him the postcard.

'Well,' said Mick, after he had read it, 'that beats me. Is the chap right in the head at all? Going round collecting false friends! And what does he want fast civil servants for?'

'Maybe we could ask Uncle Andy in Dublin,' said Pat, 'he might know. I haven't a clue. Just imagine me going round collecting civil servants. Something must have happened to poor Karl since he went back to Vienna. He used to be such a nice, normal guy!'

Suddenly Mick gripped Pat by the shoulder.

'Listen. I've got an idea. I'd love to meet that crazy friend of yours. Write back to him – if you still have his address – and tell him you'd be delighted to help him. Invite him to come here to Kiltimore. Tell him the best

English in the British Isles is spoken in Kiltimore. And promise him you'll find fifty false friends for him here.

Pat took Mick's advice, and after consulting with his parents to see if it was alright, he wrote to Karl after Christmas inviting him to Ireland. There was no reply for a long time, but shortly after Easter another postcard arrived. Karl thanked Pat for the invitation but said that at present it was impossible for him to come to Ireland because of his studies, and in summer he had to work to pay for his university fees. But he probably would have an opportunity the following year to come. However, if Pat wanted to come to Austria he was more than welcome any time. Karl added in a P.S. that he had been working hard on his false friends since Christmas and now had a collection of 144 in all.

The bit about the false friends was a complete enigma to Mick. He couldn't fathom it out. How could you collect false friends? Who were they? Did they know they were being collected?

'Listen, Pat,' he said, 'I've got an idea'

'Not again!'

'This is your chance. You always wanted to travel after leaving Gormanstown. Why don't you take him up on it? Tell him you'd be delighted to come and visit him during his summer holidays. Tell him how fond you are of Austria and how you'd love to meet some of his false friends.'

'But I can't leave the farm in the middle of all the summer work. The old man would go mad. I can't just down tools and say I'm off to Austria for a two-week holiday.'

'But,' argued Mick, '*I'll* have plenty of time to work on the farm after the Leaving Cert in June. I'll take your place.'

'No,' said Pat, 'that wouldn't do at all. Basically you

know very little about modern farming. I'm the one who's been to an agricultural college, you know. But wait a minute. I think I have a better idea!'

They looked each other in the eyes. Telepathy did the rest.

Pat: *'So you're thinking what I'm thinking ...'*

Mick: *'That's nothing strange ...'*

Pat: *'You'll go and I'll stay ...'*

Mick: *'And Karl won't know the change ...'*

Pat: *'In any case he's collecting ...'*

Mick: *'False friends by the score ...'*

Pat: *'So let's help him with his project ...'*

Mick: *'And send him on one more!'*

That very evening Pat replied to Karl, thanked him for the invitation, said he couldn't come to Austria at the present point in time because of all the ploughing and sowing that had to be done, but he probably would have an opportunity to travel sometime towards the end of the summer when the harvest was in, if that suited Karl. The two brothers made no mention of their plans at that stage to their parents, for they weren't very sure themselves if they would really go through with the scheme or not. Besides, Mick was now working very hard for his final exam in June, and hardly was Pat's letter in the post when they had both forgotten about it.

When the results of the Leaving Cert came out in August, Mr. and Mrs. Quinn were overjoyed at how well their younger son had done. Whereas Pat had just scraped through a year before in Gormanstown, Mick got A grades in all his subjects (except maths). A few evenings afterwards the family were gathered around the table for tea. The last field of hay had been cut and baled, the Massey Ferguson finally switched off and cooling down in the shed. The topic of Mick's future now came up for discussion.

'With your results, Michael, you could do medicine,' ventured Mrs. Quinn.

'I'm not very interested in becoming a doctor, and I'm not fond of the idea of going to university,' said Mick. 'What I'd like to do is travel, see the world while I'm young.'

Mr. Quinn shifted uneasily in his chair.

'Oh, you can always travel after you've finished your education,' said Mrs. Quinn. 'If you don't like medicine, you could, maybe, try engineering or accountancy.'

'But he'd want maths for those,' said Pat, with a wry smile. 'That's his worst subject!'

'What about law, then?' pressed Mrs. Quinn.

Her husband now joined in the conversation.

'Before you decide, Mick, what you're going to do next, I think you should take a break. You deserve it. Seeing that you would like to travel,' – he glanced at his wife – 'maybe you could take off somewhere for a few days, now that the work is slacking off. Of course you don't have to go on a world tour, but maybe a few days in Bundoran or Enniscrone, or even with your uncle in Dublin, would do you good. You've never been east of the Shannon up to now, have you?'

'I don't think he's mentioned it to you yet,' said Pat, but I believe Mick would like to have a holiday in Austria.'

Mick was grateful to his brother for his timely support.

Taken totally by surprise, the parents said nothing for a moment while they tried to adjust their thoughts and emotions to the new situation.

'Why Austria?' asked Mrs. Quinn, who had quickly located the country in her mind's atlas but was still struggling to come to terms with the notion of Michael not wanting to go to university. The question also gave Mr. Quinn a little time to adapt to the idea of one of his two fine sons deserting, as he said, his native sod, the Emerald

Isle, the place where he was born. A feeling associated in his heart with the emigrant's feet on Broadway fluttered about in his breast and disturbed him.

Pat explained about Karl's invitation, that Mick could go in his stead, that Karl wouldn't know the difference because the brothers were so alike, that he was collecting false friends in any case, and that Mick would probably only want to stay a week or so.

'Two at the very most,' said Mick.

Not fully understanding and still struggling to adjust, Mrs. Quinn asked:

'And what language do they speak in Austria?'

'German,' said Pat.

'And, Michael, how much German do you know?' she inquired.

'Österreich,' said Mick, and 'Aufwiedersehen'. But Pat tells me that Karl speaks English very well so there'll hardly be a problem. And I'm sure I'll pick up a few words of German while I'm there.'

Silence followed. That was that settled. The general outline of the plan was clear, only details about time, route, means of transport and finances remained to be worked out.

Pat and Mick still shared the same room, but the twin bed they slept in as children had long since been replaced by two full-size single beds at either side of the room A long writing desk beneath the window, at which there were two swivel chairs, separated the beds. A large McDonald's Books desk-mat displaying the Continents of the World covered half the desk top. When tea was over the brothers, reacting once more to an unspoken cue, made their way immediately to their room, took up positions in the swivel chairs, and, now that the prospects of one of them going there had become very real, started to look for Austria on the map. But first Mick decided to clean away the coffee stains that soiled the surface at various points. Spitting on his handkerchief, he started to rub off the dried-in grains spattered over the Atlantic and the Pacific. It was hard to know sometimes if they were in fact coffee-spots or islands. After a somewhat too scrupulous rubbing, the Galapagos Islands disappeared through a little hole west of Ecuador. However, Mauritius and Reunion and the Hawaiian Islands and Vanuatou maintained their insular presence. The romantic place names again fascinated the brothers, and each of them felt deep within him that strange longing to depart, to leave the land behind, to go and visit those wonderful, faraway places with the magic names. But for the present they had to concentrate on Austria. Returning to Europe, they saw that it was well south-east of Ireland, in a different time zone. It didn't look very big, stuck in there in the Alps between Germany and Italy.

Arrangements were soon made for Mick's journey. He booked an Aer Lingus flight to Munich at the beginning of September (the direct flights to Vienna were booked out), and a connecting train from there to the Austrian capital. Pat had got no reply to the letter he wrote to Karl after Easter. He now wrote again, giving him the details of his (actually Mick's) itinerary and enclosing a recent photo (of Mick) so that he would recognize him at the railway station in Vienna. After leaving Gormanstown he had let his hair grow again, he explained. Mick was well pleased with the plan and could hardly wait till the day of departure came.

When he was saying goodbye at the station, Mick tried to cheer his parents up by saying that he would be back in 10 days' time, or two weeks at the very most. But he did not have a return ticket. There were four or five other little groups at the station, brightly dressed and happy and gay in the warm weather of early September. Mr. Quinn wondered how anybody could be happy leaving the west of Ireland.

'Don't forget,' said Pat, slipping his brother a piece of paper with the words, 'I'm Pat, not Mick' on it, 'that from now on you're Pat!'

The train arrived ten minutes late as usual, the travellers got on, and soon the loveless diesel was pulling them away from final embraces and kisses and waving handkerchiefs. It would take them obstinately onwards over the Shannon, through the Bog of Allen, across the plains of Westmeath, Meath and Kildare and into the far-away capital. There was no one in Mick's compartment. Not thinking very much about anything in particular, he stared out unperturbed at the fields of sheep and the bogs and the lakes and the low clouds as they passed by outside his window. He was just dozing off when the train came to a jerky halt in Mullingar. Then the door of his compartment flung suddenly open and two young fellows and a girl jostled their way through together, hurraying and wobbling and hanging out of each other, and though there were plenty of seats free, they planted themselves as near as they could to the window, almost sitting on top of Mick. The girl was wearing an extraordinarily short skirt, high red boots (though the weather was warm), a ring in her nose (reminding Mick of the bull back on the farm) and another one in her tongue. 'She must be a hard one to keep in tow,' Mick thought. She sat at the window just opposite him, her bare knees actually touching his. One of her friends squeezed up very close to her. He was wearing jeans and a muscle shirt and had a green scorpion tattooed on his brawny arm. The third member of the group sat beside Mick on the bench opposite, so close that his knees pressed into Mick's thighs. Hardly had they settled when the girl took out a packet of cigarettes, ignoring the 'no smoking' sign on the wall behind her. They all lit up, then the girl looked Mick straight in the eyes and suddenly said:

'What's your name?'

'Pat, I mean Mick,' Mick floundered, caught on the hop. Then, recovering, 'My name is Michael.'

'Not even sure of his name!' said the muscle-man with a grin to his mate.

'Like a puff of nico, Micko?' said the girl, offering him a cigarette. 'I'm a friendly type, you see.' She rubbed her knees against Mick's. 'We're all friends, aren't we? All of us in this cabin here, all of us on this speedin', bleedin' train, all of us on this crazy, spinnin' globe. A Marlboro, my friend?'

'I don't smoke,' said Mick.

'Good boy,' said the girl, as she blew a billow of blue smoke right into Mick's face.

'We're off to the match in Croke Park,' said the muscle-man's mate, digging his knee deeper into Mick's thigh. Are you headin' there too?'

Mick wasn't even aware that there was a match on.

'If he is, he should have a flag,' said the girl.

Undoing the rosette with the green and white ribbons that she had pinned onto her t-shirt, she leant forward, low and erotic, to attach it to the lapel of Mick's jacket.

'Up Meath!' she then shouted, slapping him on the knee.

'As a matter of fact,' said Mick, 'I'm on my way to the airport. I'm leaving the country.'

The attitude of the friends changed dramatically.

'Coward!' said one.

'Defector!' said the second.

'Runaway!' said the third.

'Fugitive!' said the first.

'Renegade!' said the second.

'Deserter!' said the third.

Mick thought of his father's word.

Then the girl raised her hand.

'Wait,' she said, 'we're friends, aren't we? Let's not be nasty to our dear departing brother. Are you aware, Micko, that this train doesn't go to the airport?

'I know,' said Mick, 'I have to get off at Bus Áras.'

'And do you know where that is?' asked the muscle man.

'I'll know when I get there, I'm sure'

'Don't worry, mate, just relax. Bus Áras is the station before we get off!'

Grinning to his ears, he winked at his mate opposite and nudged the girl beside him. The same grin spread across their faces, too.

'That one has hair on it,' said Mick – to himself, of course.

At that stage they were joined by two other youths, each with a half-empty can of beer in one hand and a big Meath flag in the other. They were also sporting green and white crepe hats, and fans' scarves that made them sweaty and thirsty in the hot compartment. 'Up Meath and down the hatch,' they said, finishing off their beers.

Making sure that his wallet was safe in his inside pocket, Mick got off the train when he saw the Bus Áras sign. He took the bus to the airport, and as he still had an hour to wait for his flight, he strolled for a while around the Duty Free. Though he had not intended to make a purchase, he bought a hand-knit Arran pullover and a knitted woollen beret with a pom-pom to go with it, in case Karl should take him up those snow-covered Austrian mountains. He also bought a small Aer Lingus carrier bag to put them in. He liked the big green shamrock on the side. Now that he was leaving his native shore, the land of his birth, God's own country, Mick was beginning for the very first time to feel a little bit patriotic. He was himself surprised by the sentiment.

Though it was his first time to fly, Mick wasn't a bit

nervous getting on the plane. As the engines roared for take-off, he thought of the Massey Ferguson. His seat was near the window but he couldn't see out, because a lady with an enormous pink hat was leant forward completely blocking the view. She was giving what was obviously a running and enthusiastic commentary in a strange language on the changing scene outside to the quiet and terrified man beside her, no doubt her husband. When the plane reached cruising altitude, Mick could follow the route they were taking on the monitor in front of him. On they flew now south-east towards Munich, where Mick would catch the train to Vienna as planned. Suddenly he began to wonder how he would recognize Karl when he got to his destination. That hadn't occurred to him before. As a matter of fact, now that he thought of it, he wasn't even sure if Karl knew he was coming or would be there to meet him. No reply had come to Pat's last letter. But Mick didn't worry too much because if the worst came to the worst he could always take a taxi to the students' hostel where Karl was staying.

But Mick's predicament had taken a somewhat different twist without his knowing it. That afternoon, after Pat and his parents had got back home after seeing him off at the station, the postman arrived with an express letter for Pat. The Austrian stamp (Pat always found 'Österreich' ugly and unwieldy on the colourful little stamp) and the name and address of the sender written on the back of the envelope with an 'X' through it, were details that denied him the little thrill of wondering who a letter was from before opening it. (Once Pat had had a little discussion about this point with Steven the Post. When it became clear that the reason for the address on the back of the envelope was so that the letter could be returned if it couldn't be delivered, and the reason it was crossed out was so that it wouldn't be delivered straightaway to the person who wrote it, Stephen concluded that there must be an awfully efficient postal service in Austria.)

'I'm sorry, Pateen,' said Steven, handing Pat the letter with a tinge of bad conscience, 'I'm a bit late delivering it, but I've been on the broad of me back for the last three days with the 'flu. I'm still not meself yet, but I couldn't let the backlog keep piling up. The postmistress was getting very ratty, too.'

Apologising, Karl explained in his letter to Pat that since the university closed at the end of June he had first worked for a month at the furnaces in the steel works in Linz – very good pay but very hot and hard work – and then got a job in August as an usher at the Salzburg Festival. It was there that he met a beautiful American girl and they had become very good friends and were in constant contact with each other since she returned to the States, and now she had invited him to come and visit her and her family in New York where she was studying the violin at the Conservatory of Music at Brooklyn College. He was very sorry – here was the embarrassing bit – that he had to go away just when Pat planned to come to Austria, but if he didn't go in September he would have to wait till Christmas to see lovely Lorrie again. He hoped very much that Pat would understand, and he would have loved to be in Vienna to collect him, but maybe he might be still there when he got back from the United States. He needn't worry, however, about getting lost in Vienna: he had arranged for his best friend, who shared the same room with him in the hostel (and who was also called Karl, incidentally), to pick him up at the station. He could sleep in his bed, if he wanted, until he returned from the States. His friend was a very nice guy, typical Viennese. He was studying history, but his English was perfect, and he felt sure there would be no communication problems. He was very tall, about 2 metres, with a mop of red hair, and Pat would have no difficulty recognizing him. In any case he had given him Pat's photo. He signed off by apologising again and expressing the hope that his letter would arrive before he left for Austria. P.S. He was surprised Pat was flying Aer Lingus and not KLM!

Pat was disappointed with the letter. He thought his friend might have stayed on in Austria for at least a few days to welcome him. Not having any great interest himself in girls, he didn't quite see the urgency about visiting Lorrie in New York. Furthermore, what was he to do now? He couldn't contact Mick. If only they had a telephone, he could try the airport! But Mick was probably well on his way to Munich by that time in any case. He put the letter in his pocket and, whistling for Jacko, strode off across the fields to the lake to do a bit of fishing and ponder things over.

In the meantime, Mick had arrived safely in Munich. The airport bus took him to the busy Central Railway Station. He had a little over an hour to catch the train to Vienna. Everything was now in German – the ads, the names of the shops on the plastic bags people carried, the announcements over the PA. The only signs he could read were Coca Cola and Kodak. He soon realized that Munich wasn't Munich at all in Germany, but München. He had already learned from Karl's letters that Austria wasn't Austria either, but Österreich. Like his brother Pat, he disliked intensely those two dots over some letters. Maybe Vienna wasn't Vienna at all, but Vönchen or Vünreich or something like that. Not knowing which of the countless tracks his train would be leaving from, he asked a few people for directions. The first laughed at him, the second ignored him, the third answered in English, 'Sorry, pal, I'm not from here.' He took a look at the train timetable on the electronic board, but it was so complicated and foreign that he could make neither head nor tail of it. He decided to try his luck down one of the platforms where a train stood waiting. With his Aer Lingus bag on his arm, he was steering his suitcase along on its wobbly wheels when he noticed the station clock over his head. He glanced at his watch – he was an hour slow! Then he suddenly realized he was in a different time zone. He sprinted forward to the waiting train. Out of one of the windows hung a large green and white flag with the words 'RAPID WIEN' written on it – could it possibly be the express to Vienna? He ran towards the window and shouted 'Vienna? Vienna?' A porter passing behind him said 'Ja, ja. Yes, yes' and walked on. Mick saw that the train was jammed full and he began to lose heart. He tried in vain to open the door. Then a huge red face leered out at him and a muscular arm pressed down the handle from the inside. The door opened and he was pulled unceremoniously in, bag and baggage. Swallowed up in a sea of bodies, he saw the door close automatically behind him. The electric train started imperceptibly to glide away down the track on its long, long journey to the Austrian capital. Dead on time!

Jammed tight like the proverbial sardine, Mick tried to take his bearings. All he could see about him was green and white shirts, flags, scarves and hats. Some faces were even painted green and white. Football fans again! 'Am I on my way to Vienna or Croke Park?' he asked himself. The noise deafened his ears. Everybody had to shout to be heard, so it got louder and louder. There was nobody without a can of Heineken or Beck's or Kronbacher in his hand, some had carrier packs of 6 in their arms. And of course Mick didn't understand a word, it all being in German. He was tired now, and hungry, and would like to have got sitting down, but trying to force his way through that phalanx of fans with his case was too daunting a task. Then somebody saw the green and white rosette in Mick's lapel. And somebody else pointed to the green shamrock on his carrier-bag. A can of beer was pressed into his hand and a very heavy and tattooed arm leaned heavily on his shoulders. Those about him raised their beers, Mick his, and it was 'prost!' and 'cheers' and 'cheerio' everywhere. And down the hatch at one go. Three or four started talking to Mick at the same time but he understood nothing. Someone in the second row who had a smattering of English said, 'You from England?' 'No,' said Mick, 'Ireland.' They did not understand. 'Wo?' they repeated to each other, 'Wo? Wo? Wo?' It reminded Mick of what the farmers at home said when trying to bring a horse or donkey to a halt. They shrugged their shoulders and put another beer in Mick's hand. Mick turned around to the window behind him that was all steamed up and spelled Ireland on the glass with his beery fingers. The penny dropped somewhere in the crowd and an enlightened voice shouted louder than the others: 'Ah, Irland!' Then they all re-echoed 'Irland' knowingly, and they embraced him and slapped him on the back again, and sputtered sprays of Bavarian beer down his neck. Then the one with the smattering said, 'You from Irland, you Ire!' 'Pardon me?' said Mick. 'You Ire?!' the other repeated. Mick thought he was saying 'eerie'. Then someone else said 'Irrer, nicht Ire.' That really set the flames of hilarity blazing. They laughed and sputtered and coughed and choked and lost their breaths at the humour of it. If it had been physically possible, some of them would surely have fallen over with the laughing. Mick did not quite get the point of the joke but, he thought to himself, I suppose 'eerie' is a funny word. He started laughing, too, and once he had started he couldn't stop, and within a few seconds he had one arm across his neighbours' shoulders saying 'Irrer, nicht Ire' too. It was such a terribly funny word, really, it had never struck him before. Then he got an idea. Laying his case flat, he stood up on it, raised his hand for silence, took his

113

wallet out of his pocket and called out, 'A round of drinks on the Irrer nicht Ire!' He forgot he was not in a pub and there was no bartender. But they didn't understand him anyway, so it made no difference. He found himself with the next can of beer in his hand, and once more it was straight down the hatch. Then the fellow with the few words of English came slobbering right up into Mick's face and stuck his thick thumb on the rosette in his lapel. 'You Rapid fan, us Rapid fans'. Mick had no idea what 'rapeed' meant. He kissed both of Mick's hands, embraced him passionately but unsteadily, repeating over and over again, 'You Rapid fan, you my friend!' Then he started singing loudly into Mick's ear, and soon they were all singing together in various keys. They swayed to and fro, the beer frothed and overflowed and spread stains on their shirts and jeans. They tried to lift Mick onto their shoulders, but he couldn't cooperate: so much drink on an empty stomach was beginning to have its effect on him. The din and the discord, the bad air, the heat of the place, the rhythm of the train and the spiky German language jolting like little electric shocks through his brain, took their inevitable toll. He was out cold before the train reached Rosenheim.

Mick came slowly to in the early hours of the morning on a cold railway station bench in the half-deserted hall of the West Railway Station in Vienna. His head was spinning and his eyes hurt. The hazy outline of the morning sun shining in on him through a high window slowly focused into the clear outline of a mop of red hair. A very tall man was looking down on him from the sky. 'Welcome, my friend, to Austria,' he said. Mick jolted upright. He automatically shot his hand into his inside pocket. His passport and wallet were gone. All he found was Pat's slip of paper reminding him he was Pat now. And his case? That was gone, too! Only the carrier bag with the Arran sweater was

114

still there. The rosette lay in shreds beneath the bench, almost unrecognisable.

'I'm Karl,' said the very tall man, proffering Mick his hand.

Mick grabbed his bag and was about to flee.

'Wait,' said Karl, 'Don't run away. I'm a friend. I'm here to collect you!'

Befuddled though his mind still was, the stranger's next words arrested his flight.

'You're Pat, from Ireland, aren't you?' said Karl.

He presented the photo Pat had sent. That was convincing enough. The panic began to subside and he regained his composure somewhat.

'I think you got Karl's letter?' said Karl.

Mick, of course, knew nothing about the letter Pat had got the day he left. Suspicions came creeping slowly back. This couldn't be the Karl who was in Gormanstown with Pat. This beanpole with the shock of flaming red hair must be someone else. But the photo?

'No, I didn't,' said Mick. Then he thought of his lost property, vaguely remembered other friends he had met on his way. He grew even more suspicious.

'Would you have any idea where my case and my missing wallet and passport are?' he ventured to ask.

'I'm afraid you got into bad company on the train, Pat. I saw a few of the Rapid fans (again 'rapeed') deposit you on the bench there after getting off. You're lucky they didn't strip you naked!'

Pat had only hazy recollections of the train journey from Munich. He looked at the slip of paper in his hand, 'I'm Pat, not Mick.' He glanced up at red Karl, thinking to himself, 'And he's not Karl either. Why did he say he was?' But when Karl offered to take him back to the hostel in his car and give him a good breakfast, Pat began to warm up towards him. He hadn't much choice, anyway, but to trust the man, though he swore to himself he was going to be very careful from now on about who he was going to make friends with. After breakfast, Karl told Pat not to worry about money, because he could lend him some. Later he took him to the Irish Embassy to report the stolen passport and apply for a new one. However, that wasn't such an easy matter: they had to check things out with the Department of Foreign Affairs in Dublin and it could take up to three weeks for a new passport to be issued. Pat was glad that he had not bought a return ticket.

Sat that afternoon at a sidewalk café on the Kärntnerstrasse (two niggling dots), the main street in Vienna, Mick brought up the question again with Karl about the letter.

'I didn't get any letter from you,' said Mick, remembering he was Pat.

'No, not from me,' said Karl, 'from the other Karl, Karl Mittag.'

'Oh, so you're not the Gormanstown Karl?' said Mick, catching on fast.

'No,' said Karl, 'I've never been to Ireland. I'm Karl's friend. We just happen to have the same name. My family name is Müller. Karl is a very common name in Austria.'

He showed Mick his student's identity card. (The two dots were becoming a plague). Realizing now that, like himself, Karl wasn't who he was supposed to be, Mick began to feel on safer ground.

'I was thinking you couldn't be the Flyer I knew in college.'

Karl was very surprised that his friend's letter to Pat hadn't arrived, so he explained again about the girlfriend in New York, and why the 'true' Karl wasn't there to collect him. Mick tried to make the best of it, but he was very disappointed because he had been so looking forward to meeting him and all his false friends. He wondered if this Karl knew anything about them, was perhaps even one of them. He began to grow suspicious again. He'd bide his time, play it by ear.

Karl turned out to be a very likeable guy, with a lot of understanding. He knew how Mick must have been feeling after his trial by train, as he called it, so after showing him St. Steven's Cathedral at one end of the Kärntnerstrasse and the Opera House and Burg Theater on the Ring, he suggested they return to the hostel in the Josephstadt District and relax.

'Tomorrow I'll show you around a bit, take you out into the Vienna Woods perhaps, go on one of the walking tours in the city, show you the Beethoven and Strauss memorials. I'm sure you'd enjoy it. Do you like Strauss?'

All Mick knew about Strauss was what was printed in tiny letters on the postcard Pat had got from Karl the previous Christmas.

'Oh yes,' said Mick, 'he's a great fiddler indeed!'

Karl thought Mick extremely funny, and Mick had got to like Karl more and more as the day went on. That night Mick slept in the missing Karl's bed in the hostel, and in the morning put on his Arran and the hand-knitted woollen beret with the pom-pom. After breakfast they set out on the tour.

The weather had changed. A cold easterly wind was now blowing in through the city from the Great Hungarian Plain. Mick's apparel occasioned furtive glances and an odd disapproving smirk from some well-dress citizens of the upper Viennese echelons. Karl was a very good guide, he knew Vienna like his 'waistcoat pocket', as he said. After three hours of churches and undergrounds and museums and palaces, Mick's mind was fairly boggled. His feet, too, were hurting because he had to take three steps to every two of Karl's long strides. He was more than relieved when mid-day came and Karl invited him to the

Augustinerkeller for lunch. After a pint of wonderful Ottakringer ale, Mick's mood greatly improved. Karl was in the best of spirits, too, and now the time seemed ripe for Mick to gingerly broach the subject of Karl's false friends. He took an indirect approach.

'Vienna is lovely,' he said, 'but when we were in Gormanstown Karl once showed us a video with farmhouses and steep sloping hills and high mountains covered with snow. I'd love to see the agricultural side of Austria. Any chance, do you think?'

'Well, I'm not the right man for that, I'm afraid,' said Karl. I'm a city slicker through and through. I've never been further west than Linz. I'm afraid you'll have to wait till Karl gets back to see those parts.'

'When is he coming back?' asked Mick.

'God only knows. He seems to have fallen head over heels in love with Lorrie from Broadway. Maybe he'll never come back!'

Mick could hear his father singing, 'My feet are here on Broadway'.

'Wouldn't his friends miss him very much?' asked Mick, insinuatingly.

'He hasn't got very many friends, really. As you probably know, he's an orphan and lives with his grandmother up in the hills south of Salzburg. His parents were killed in an avalanche. Here in Vienna, I'm the only real friend he has.'

'Maybe he's got some false friends,' Mick thrusted.

'False friends!' said Karl, astonished. 'What makes you think that?'

Mick decided to reveal what Karl himself had mentioned in his letters.

'He even seems to be collecting them,' said Mick. 'He had 144 by the last count.'

At first completely nonplussed, Karl then did recollect

vaguely that he had once seen some notes and a False Friend file lying around on his friend's desk but he had not given it any special attention. He though it was some project or other he was doing at the Uni.

'Yes,' said Mick, 'I think it was some kind of project.'

Karl called for the bill, the waiter came, Karl paid, and then they continued, regaled, on their walking tour of the city.

As he was lying on the bed that evening, exhausted from all the walking and new impressions and extraordinary sights and people rushing here and there and nowhere, Mick's eye scanned the bookshelf over his head and discovered just what he hoped might be in the room somewhere: the False Friends file.

'Do you think,' he asked Karl, 'it would be alright if we had a peep inside the file?'

He felt he might be intruding on the author's privacy, and he was also a little apprehensive about what might be in the file. Supposing, for instance, Karl the red-head was listed as one of the false friends! It was better if he had his support. The latter was stretching his long legs out on the other bed across the room.

'There can't be much harm in having a look,' he reassured Mick. He was wondering himself who all those false friends could be.

They sat beside each other at the long desk under the window. Karl opened the file. There were lists in it alright, many pages with words arranged in alphabetical order. Each entry had a number. But there were no names, no addresses, no telephone numbers – just words, lists of words. Karl read out the first three entries under 'A':

absolvieren	$\neq$	*absolve*
also	$\neq$	*also*
Angel	$\neq$	*angel*

'I don't get it,' said Pat. 'Is it coded?'

Karl suddenly covered his face in his hands, buried his fingers in his thick hair and began to chuckle to himself.

'What an idiot am I! How could I be so stupid!'

Then he explained to Pat that the German word *absolvieren* looked very like the English word *absolve* but it didn't have the same meaning at all. In the case of *also* and *Angel* it was even worse, because the words were spelt exactly the same way in German and English but they had very different meanings.

'Such words are called 'false friends' because they can be very misleading. Now I remember,' said Karl. 'We were taught that many years ago in school. I had completely forgotten.'

'I see,' said Mick. He paused for a moment. Then he said:

'Let's have a look under 'F''

The first three entries under 'F' were:

fad	≠	*fad*
fast	≠	*fast*
Fee	≠	*fee*

Pat looked closely at *fast*. The penny was on its way down.

'I wonder if 'civil servant' is in the file, he said to Karl.

'A civil servant without a file?' quipped Karl. 'That's hardly possible! But that old chestnut I can explain myself. 'Civil' in English is 'zivil' in German, and 'servant' in English is 'Diener' in German. However, a 'civil servant' is not a 'Zivildiener' but a 'Beamte'.

'And what is a Zivildiener?', asked Mick.

'A young man who does community service instead of the compulsory military service.'

The penny finally dropped. So Karl's fast civil servants were only words, ideas, and did not exist in reality.

'Did you really think they did?' asked Karl.

Later Karl got dressed up and went out on his own to the

cinema, Mick having decided to stay in because he was tired. The wind had chopped his lips and reddened his face, and in any case he was penniless. Before putting Karl's file back on the shelf, he turned over the pages and went to the last entry, no. 144. It read:

Ton   ≠   *ton*

Then taking a pencil he added as no. 145:

Rapid   ≠   *rapid*

Later he wrote a long letter home to Pat, giving him a detailed account of everything that had happened, explaining to him the riddle of the false friends, and asking him to send on a little money to tide him over. 'So you see,' he finished off,

'there are many false friends about, no matter where you go;

but Karl's, at least, are helpful, and have taught me what I know:

that Munich is called München, and Vienna here is Wien,

and Rapid is the name of a football team, and it's pronounced 'rapeed';

and German angels aren't angels at all, and a ton is not a weight,

and civil servants are community workers, and – for the next word you'll have to wait

till I see the colour of your money!

Your 'friend in need, indeed!'

Mick.'

THE NOBEL PRIZE

Micky, an Irishman exiled on the cold continent, was seated uncomfortably in the plush armchair in the centre. Right of him was his Austrian wife, Martha, left of him his German friend, Manfred. Their chairs were harder than his, though they also had armrests. A small group of people – journalists, TV-reporters, two cameramen, public representatives, friends, acquaintances – had gathered in the cosy baroque salon, with its rich, golden ornamentation, its stately portraits of past city mayors, its modern landscape watercolours of purple mountains, red sunsets and white fields of winter snow and frost, to pay tribute to Micky.

Micky, the true Irish exile, ardently loved his native land. Funnily enough, the longer he was away from it, the more ardently he seemed to love it. On that May morning five years before – despite the fact that, as poets required, the birds were singing, the lambs dancing about in the meadows, the salmon leaping upstream and the bees buzzing among the flower-beds – not a tear did he shed as he departed from Erin's green shore. As a matter of fact, the last words he said to his brother as he got on the boat were, 'When will you cop on and leave this bloody country, too?'

But five years had brought many changes in Micky's life. He had, he wrote to his brother, settled down in Austria, found a job, bought a car, taken a wife, built a house, made many friends – and a major discovery. A shrewd and observant countryman, he soon came to realize that in the competitive world of business, banks, booms and bankruptcies he had one great advantage abroad, one asset he never knew he possessed, one trump card he would have remained completely unaware of, had he remained in the west of Ireland. Micky's mother language was English, and every second person he met in Austria seemed to want to learn English, or improve their English, or just talk to him in English. Without any effort of his own, he grew in importance, like the last egg in the fridge. By and large, it turned out to be a pleasant discovery, tolerably profitable, and he decided to stay. But that was the decision that had landed him ultimately in this present uncomfortable predicament. He longed for the next ten minutes to pass quickly.

He turned his head and looked at Martha. She was listening courteously to what the City Mayor was saying at the rostrum. Great achievement. New insights. Salzburg is proud. Great things can be expected. Her green eyes were smiling under the festive lights. They were the emerald link that first attracted Micky to her, though in fact he had expected Austrian girls' eyes (or was it German girls' eyes?) to be blue. He could never look in her eyes without thinking of Ireland. One warm Sunday afternoon in September, early in their courtship, Micky was sitting with Martha on the veranda of a city centre restaurant, looking out over the river. Was it the mild Wachau wine from Lower Austria? Was it the waters of the Salzach flowing, forever faithful, to their rendezvous with the Inn at Braunau? Or was it – more likely – the fact that just then the All Ireland Final was on in Dublin and he had not missed it once in twenty years? At any rate, he grew nostalgic. But unwary, too.

'Somehow I wish you had blue eyes,' he said to Martha, 'it would make things easier now. Your green ones are making me homesick!'

He didn't mean any harm, but the remark was misguided.

'I'm sorry,' she said, 'first thing tomorrow I'll go and have them dyed. Which would you like, navy or sky?'

And off she went, in high dudgeon. 'Oh, the seriousness of these central Europeans,' Micky thought, and almost took the next train north to the coast.

But their love had weathered that storm.

He turned to look at Manfred, on his left. Manfred, from Nuremberg, did indeed have bright blue German eyes, and they were now fixed on the Councillor for Culture, who had taken the place of the Mayor at the rostrum. It was Manfred, his best friend, his most obliging neighbour, his supplier of paint and paint brushes and wine and good advice, Manfred, his English pupil, his worldly-wise philosopher, his admirer and provoker, Manfred, the company director and the man with ever such good contacts, the man who organized trips to Brazil and London and China for his paint customers, who had got him into this embarrassing situation. Manfred, and his accomplice – Martha!

It had all begun with a simple, one-way bet in Manfred's house one Saturday evening the year before. Having got through another chapter of *The African Queen*, they put the book aside. Micky was bored by the simplified version, but at least it was helping Manfred improve his English. They tipped their small Lufthansa glasses (justified souvenirs of an expensive business trip to Brazil), glanced into each other's eyes as ceremony required, said 'Prost!', and drank off the remaining Green Veltliner. They felt contented. Through the large, double-glazed windows enclosing the rectangular patio that Manfred had added to his house shortly after he was appointed National Sales Manager, Austria, for Akzo Nobel's Sikkens Paints, shone millions of bright, clear, November stars. They sparkled and twinkled above the prickly tops of the pine trees that stood stiff with cold in the garden. There were little clusters of white, yellow and pale blue frost-crystals on the broad glass pane. But inside it was warm, and the glowing logs on the red brick hearth kept the bitterly-cold airs of the Alps well at bay. It was a night to be in.

'One for the road!' said Manfred, very secure now in the phrase he had practised at this stage of the lesson for months. His sensitive fingers were already closing in on the Gothic spire and the cluster of grapes depicted on the label of the bottle. Micky noticed that his hand trembled a little.

'And what about your book?' Manfred said, as he poured the final glass.

That, too, had become a regular phrase at their Saturday evening sessions. Once, a month or two before, when he was particularly bored by *The African Queen* but had found abundant consolation in five glasses of Manfred's white wine, Micky had remarked in an unguarded moment that he could write a better book himself. Manfred picked him up on it, and ever since had been teasing him and challenging him and provoking him and encouraging him to write a book. Now apart from filling in registration forms and applications for residence permits and building grants, Micky's compositional exercises up to that point had been confined to the occasional letter home to the brother. He was beginning to regret his literary bravado – why do central Europeans have to take a joke seriously? – when Manfred repeated the question.

'Okay, okay,' said Micky, 'stop taking the mickey out of me!' (Ha, he won't understand that!) 'I'll write a book. I'll write a better book than *The African Queen*. But only on one condition.'

'Which is?' said Manfred.

'That you paint a nice picture. Selling Akzo Nobel

paints to decorate houses and office blocks and insurance company buildings is all very well. But why don't you go and do some painting yourself. Artistic painting, I mean, not just decorating. You paint a nice picture and I'll write a nice book.'

'Oh,' replied Manfred, 'I've painted lots of nice pictures – using the very best Van Gogh paints from Switzerland.'

This could only be another of Manfred's flights of fancy. Micky had often lingered on after the lesson to listen to his friend's business-trip tales about the woman the Russian mafia set on him in Turkey, or the rows of new office blocks on the London docks he had provided the paint for but were now occupied only by squatters, or the inglorious retreat (in his underpants) of a respectable Carinthian schoolmaster from a basement room in Soho on another business trip to London, or the rejuvenating effects the ginseng root had on a 92-year old farmer friend in Korea, or how his Bavarian hat was blown off as he stood on the Great Wall of China and how the air hostess handed it to him (without the feather) as he was about to board his plane again in Shanghai. But never had Manfred given the slightest hint that he painted pictures.

'Seeing is believing,' said Micky, calling his bluff.

'Come with me,' said Manfred, as he emptied his glass.

He led Micky trundling after him from the patio back in through the living-room and out to the garage on the other side of the house. He switched on a dim light, mooched around behind the Audi and nearly broke his neck over the children's skis lying in the corner. From under an old blanket he produced a rectangular canvas with frayed edges and no frame. Micky saw splashes of bright yellows and greens, and trees and leaves, and a black-brown path leading nowhere, and a rolling mass of dark blue that seemed in the weak light of the dusty garage to be the ocean in storm. Manfred produced three of four more similar works and then discarded them in the corner, not even bothering to cover them up again. Micky could not tell how many he had altogether.

'Now,' said Manfred triumphantly, 'what about your book?'

The gauntlet was down. The joke was now on Micky. He just shrugged his shoulders, knowing well that he would never write a book. Not that he didn't have plenty of yellow and blue and green ideas himself, but it was organising them and getting them down on paper that awed him. And basically he was bone idle. Still he felt ill at ease, disgruntled, upstaged. He didn't want to give in to Manfred that easily. And somehow he was aware of an ugly undertone in what he said next.

'I'll write my book if you paint a masterpiece!'

It was a stupid thing to say, but Manfred cleverly chose to ignore it and countered succinctly:

'I'll bet you'll never write a book. I'll give you the best bottle of wine I have in my cellar, a 1935 vintage Veronese Valpolicella, if you write a book of any kind – good, bad or indifferent.'

The latter was another of those phrases Manfred had learned well and liked to use. He now turned it back nicely to plague the man who had taught it to him.

Walking back the fifty metres to his own home, Micky couldn't help feeling like a fish on a hook. Was it Manfred's excellent salesmanship that had caught him? – that natural unschooled talent for understanding the workings of other men's minds that made him the most successful seller of paint in the whole of Austria? Still feeling shabby, he decided that he preferred Green Veltliner to Valpolicella in any case, and dismissed the incident with another shrug of his shoulders. He fumbled for his keys in the cold, then entered his own cosy kitchen where Martha was browsing through a mail-order catalogue, two unnecessary copies of which had been stuffed into the mailbox by the frozen fingers of the Pakistani boy anxious to get his rounds over quickly. Micky soon recovered his composure through the effects of the warm kitchen and the good wine. When Martha looked up at him with a loving smile, she reminded him of Edna O'Brien's *Girl With Green Eyes*, the next book he planned to do with Manfred after *The African Queen*. On their way upstairs, Martha announced to Micky that her mother had rung inviting them for lunch the next day in Linz.

'And she told you not to forget your flute,' said Martha, with a twinkle in her eye.

'Indeed I won't,' said Micky. 'After Mass we'll hit the highway. Hope there's no snow or ice.'

'And there's a Chagall exhibition on in the Lenzia Gallery, too. We might go there, if we have time,' said Martha. 'I love Chagall!'

Micky had never been to a painting exhibition.

The next day the sun was shining. The snow ploughs had cleared away the few centimetres of snow that had fallen overnight. The treacherous film of ice beneath had melted under the swathes of salt spread by the rotors of the autobahn clearance trucks – the salt that Micky cursed when he saw in spring the damage it had done to the chassis of his car. But the surface was dry and safe and as he drove along his mind soon drifted away to the first time he drove the 120 Kilometres from Salzburg to Linz with Martha. Micky was very fond of Martha's parents, and they of him. His mother-in-law always made 'drunken Capuchin' for him as dessert – a lovely, light, brown, spongy cake saturated in hot, white wine. His father-in-law cooked the main meal – a schnitzel or a steak, with lots of greens. 'Full of vitamins,' he used to say, but Micky hated uncooked vegetables. 'I'm not a rabbit,' he would say in

128

jest, 'and I don't like vitamins.' The quaint Irishman was always expected to be a bit different, ever since that first time he turned up with Martha in their house wearing a fawn, hand-knit, woollen tam with a pom-pom on it, an Arran cardigan, and red flannel trousers, with a tin whistle sticking out of the hip pocket. He always had to play '*The Last Rose of Summer*' for them after lunch. That tradition had started very unexpectedly the first time they met. Micky was delighted at their interest in Irish music, and was glad to render '*The Connaughtman's Rambles*' and '*Miss McCleod's Reel*' and '*The Boys of Blue Hill*'. Martha then gave a hint that that was perhaps enough of that kind of music for the time being, so he switched to a more plaintive medley that included '*Danny Boy*' and '*Oft in the Stilly Night*' and '*It Will not be Long Dear till our Wedding Day*'. When he moved into '*The Last Rose of Summer*' there was a short gasp of surprise and a little simultaneous shriek of delight from both of Martha's parents. Micky stopped.

'Oh, that's lovely,' her mum said, 'that's from Flotow. *Martha* is our favourite opera. That's why we called our only daughter 'Martha'. Beautiful. Sorry for interrupting. Please continue.'

Micky was somewhat nonplussed, never having heard of Flotow, but the effect was very positive and contributed, he felt sure, to the readiness with which he was accepted by them when he later asked for their daughter's hand in marriage.

He was looking forward very much to lunch, and was in very high spirits as they entered the driveway to the house where Martha's parents lived.

Everything went according to plan – the schnitzel, the drunken Capuchin, The Last Rose of Summer – and the coffee was now gurgling in the percolator when a garrulous aunt of Martha's arrived unexpectedly in a fur coat and told of the progress her budgie was making, for he could now say 'pretty boy' and 'shut up' as clear as could be, and she took a tape from her bag with a recording she had made of the budgie, and she put the tape on and the budgie's voice was heard loud and clear by all, especially the aunt, saying the said words over and over again, with intermissions of other sounds that weren't quite so intelligible and required a little interpretation for those who weren't concentrating properly, and she continued breathlessly with a very funny story that the woman who was sat beside her on the bus on the tour she had made through the South Tyrol and Lombardy and Veneto – the best wine she ever tasted, though she was not a wine drinker as such, was in a little bar near the ponte Pietra in Verona – had told her about how she and her husband had got lost in the mountains when they were on holidays in Mexico the year before and had to spend two nights on the Sierra Madre in a volcanic cone. Taking advantage of a brief interval, Martha nipped in very adroitly, gave the beck to Micky, explained that they had better be leaving immediately for the Chagall exhibition, as it was closing at 5 pm and otherwise it would not be worth their while going there. Then she and Micky took their sudden leave as Martha's trapped parents were being introduced to the latest cure for the gout.

Chagall meant little to Micky. They browsed around the gallery for a while, avoiding the guided groups. They preferred no to be told anything about the paintings, at least not before they got their own impressions. Micky was a little confused by the strange figures flying over cities with bags on their backs, or standing beheaded behind red cows. But he liked the colours. Most of all he was taken by Chagall's goat, which seemed to turn up in some form or other in every picture. Memories of what his father used to call 'goats' pills' back in Roscommon flicked through his mind. When he came to *The Dream*, Micky stopped dead in his tracks. He started to chuckle, then he laughed out loud. Martha dug her elbow in his ribs – to no avail. She moved away from him, embarrassed, and contemplated *The Green Jew* on the opposite wall. Micky's laughter subsided gradually as he became aware of censorious looks and dark frowns. But how could he explain, to Martha or to anybody else? He was thinking of a tape he had bought on his honeymoon, *A Feast of Irish Folk*. One song in particular. First there is a speaker. He introduces Julia. She is playing the bodhran. The speaker refers to her as *Bean ar bhuinn gabhail*, the *Woman on the goat*. And there in *The Dream* was the same thing again: a woman in a green and red dress, breasts exposed, stretched supine on the back of an embarrassed red goat in a purple sky. It was just too funny. On the way back to Salzburg Micky asked Martha out of the blue:

'When did Chagall live?'

Martha wasn't sure.

'Do you think he had the tape, too?'

'I have no notion what you're talking about,' she said. 'These Celts are always talking in riddles,' she thought to herself.

The following Saturday morning Manfred was in the driveway with his easel and his very best Van Gogh paints from Switzerland. He was putting the finishing touches to a canvas when Micky stopped by. The sun was shining bright and cold, which made the wet oils look even more brilliant. No particular motif was apparent in the picture from close range, but when Micky stepped back from it a little he thought he could distinguish two violet lips in the dark blue clouds that whirled clockwise across the top half of the painting from left to right. The clouds developed into strong green-blue waters as they moved down into the lower half and rolled in the opposite direction. Where they encountered the solid earth at the bottom, a very bright surge of impressive yellow curled up through the middle of the picture, its broad band tapering into a swung streak to form a kind of eye in the centre. The left-hand side of the canvas was given to more peaceful ochres and greens that suggested forests and paths and fallen leaves.

'That's really nice,' said Micky. 'Is that your master-piece?'

'Masterpiece?' said Manfred, 'it's just rubbish. But I like to be out in the fresh air, I'm enjoying myself.'

'What do you do with your pictures?' Micky asked, thinking of the ones he had seen in the corner of the garage. 'Do you sell them?'

'I give them away to anyone who wants them,' said Manfred. 'This one is for the city mayor. He was here a while ago looking for a few cans of paint to do up his house. He liked it. He said as Lord Mayor he never knew when an occasion might come up where he could make good use of it. The next one is yours, if you want.'

'Thanks very much,' said Micky, 'but I'm not really into painting, though some pictures can be quite amusing.' But he couldn't explain the Chagall experience to Manfred, either.

Micky felt that Manfred's paintings were pointing a finger at him.

That evening at the lesson no mention was made of the paintings. Nor – for the first time in months – did Manfred say to Micky, 'And your book?' There was something between them now, something unconsciously at work beneath the surface. They both felt it.

It continued like that all through the winter. Then one stormy Saturday evening towards the end of March, when the frost and snow had almost departed and the grass was beginning to turn from a wintry brown to a new fresh green, Micky arrived on Manfred's patio at 8pm as usual, only this time he planted a pile of sheets on the little round table where the two Lufthansa glasses stood by the Gothic church and the grapes.

'There's my book,' he said to Manfred.

All through the cold months of November, December, January, February and March, Micky had returned Saturdays from Manfred to Martha under the influence of wine, which usually prompted Martha to retire early. But what was first only a circumstance eventually became an opportunity and Micky, left on his own in the kitchen, had started, just for the fun of it, jotting down points and making notes of what had happened during the week, of little things he had noticed, of delightful Austrian customs, of dress and manners and that were very different to Ireland. He was amused to see his neighbour have the engine of his car washed in the garage. He couldn't believe it that nobody stirred from his seat after Mass on Sunday until the priest was back in the sacristy. He loved the traditional dresses with the colourful, hand-embroidered patterns and breast-enhancing stays that women of all ages wore on special occasions, though it took him some time to realize that the apron that invariably went with the dresses had nothing at all to do with the kitchen. He admired the punctuality of the buses and trains, the wonderful autobahn system, the cleanliness of the people, the houses, almost of the very fields. The selection – and availability at any time! – of restaurant foods (and wines) was a constant source of wonderment to him. Order was everywhere, people abided by the rules. Sometimes it went too far, like the time the policeman fined him for crossing the street when the pedestrian light was red, though there wasn't a vehicle of any kind in view for miles. And the snow in winter, the lakes in summer, the friendliness of the people! He made little records of whatever came into his head, at random, without much plan or order. When he finally went to bed his mind would continue working while he was asleep, with the result that he often had the brightest ideas the next day at Mass while the priest was giving the sermons he couldn't understand. And so it came to pass that at the end of March he had a whole collection of wine-and-sermon sheaves, twelve separate little bundles, each held together with weak paper clips, and these he now presented to Manfred and claimed his Valpolicella.

As he went downstairs to the cellar to get the precious wine, Manfred felt something similar to that sweet satisfaction of the salesman who has lost all the arguments but gained a valuable customer. They opened the bottle, and as their glasses clinked Manfred asked:

'And is that *your* masterpiece?'

'Masterpiece! It's just rubbish,' Micky replied.

They laughed, and took another sip of wine.

'And what will I do with this 'African Queen' of yours?' asked Manfred, eyeing the pages he had no intention ever of reading.

'Throw it in the fire there,' said Micky, 'and watch the blue and yellow flames flare up and die away. They might provide more inspiration!'

They finished the bottle of red Valpolicella, which Micky did not at all like, and *The African Queen*, which was a great relief to him. The following Saturday they would begin with *Girl With Green Eyes*.

On Monday, Manfred rang Martha while Micky was at work. Wasn't she an English-German translator? Would she do it? It might succeed! He had very good contact with a rich publisher in Salzburg, a red-haired lady, very ugly really, who very much appreciated the painting he had given her to comfort her when she got divorced, and said she would be glad to do him a favour if ever the occasion arose. Well, this might be the occasion now. He would send her one of the stories. But it must all very secret and on no account was Micky to get wind of it.

Martha's lips were sealed. She worked hard and fast. They had no children at that stage so she had plenty of time. The red-haired publisher read the first story, was delighted (genuinely), couldn't wait to read the second one, and when she had received and read the last one she made up her mind. She printed two thousand copies and submitted the work for the *Salzburg's Best Young Author* prize. It was short-listed first, then won the award. When Micky did get wind of it and the whole truth finally came out, things had gone too far. So here he was, profoundly uncomfortable in a plush armchair, wishing he had never left home.

The Mayor was beckoning him to the rostrum. Micky went forward, said a few words, thanked everybody he could think of, read a passage, gave autographs, was ceremoniously kissed by a blue-eyed blonde in traditional costume, got a magnificent bouquet of embarrassing flowers, was clapped and photographed and interviewed. Then his prize was rolled in gently on a trolley, artistically supported on either side by the maiden arms of two other blondes in traditional costumes. They delicately removed the braided ribbons and decorous cretonne, confounded momentarily when the cellotape stuck perversely to the side of the frame. In the applause that then followed the successful unmasking, Micky seemed to be the only one who realized that the painting was upside down: the yellow band tapering into an eye should be at the bottom instead of the top. He tried to catch Manfred's eye, but he was busy explaining something to Martha.

'My Nobel Prize!' Micky reflected, as the applause began to die away.

GIVING GOD A HAND

It was a Wednesday afternoon. The term was coming to a close. A pile of test papers lay on my desk, waiting to be corrected. 'Come, Holy Spirit,' I prayed, glancing at the print of Henriques' *Pentecost* on the wall.

There was a gentle knock at my door.

'Come in!'

'I'm Elsa Barroso, from Portugal. I'm in your translation class.'

'Yes, I know.'

'I've got a problem, sir.'

A problem. Oh, yes. Indeed. A problem. Nothing new. Students are always having problems. What is it this time? Was ill during the exam? The text was very difficult? Can't be here for the repeats? I looked in her dark, southern eyes. A problem. A Portuguese girl with a problem. That's new. A Portuguese problem? Portuguese – that romantic word fluttered around in my mind for a moment. It set a little bell tinkling. Far away on the hazy outskirts of my memory a cluster of sleepy recollections awoke to the sound. They floated slowly into the clear centre of my consciousness and soon I was on the wing, away out of my office, gliding swiftly to the south, away from the isles, across the Alps, down over Spain and Portugal itself, over the Sahara and into the white sun of West Africa. I arrived at Umuezoka School, ten thousand and two days before, ten minutes to the bell for the end of the English class. The last exercise.

'Linus, what are the people from France called?'

'The French, sir'

'And a man from France?'

'A Frenchman, sir.'

'Very good. Mongo, what are the people from Spain called?'

'The Spanish, sir.'

'And what is a man from Spain called?'

'A Spaniard, sir.'

'Excellent. Ngugi, what are the people from Portugal called?'

'The Portuguese, sir.'

'And what is a man from Portugal called?'

A slight hesitation, then

'A Portugoose, sir.'

So long ago!

'Well, Miss, how can I help you?'

'It's about my end-of-term certificate, sir. My Professor back in Lisbon said I have to submit it to him by next Monday at the very latest. Could I have it, please, by Friday. I'm flying home on Saturday.'

'But,' I said, 'I have to correct your examination script first before I can issue you a certificate with a grade on it. As you can see, I have lots and lots of examination papers to correct. Today is Wednesday. How could you possibly expect me to have the results by the day after tomorrow? And it's not just the correcting: there's a lot of other work involved. I have to check the grades achieved in term papers, I have to confer with my colleagues, I have to keep records. And I have so many other things to do besides.'

The old wrestling game had started again.

'I'm afraid your Professor in Lisbon will just have to wait.'

Elsa grew nervous.

'I telephoned with him today, sir. He said if I don't hand in the certificate by Monday – with a positive grade! – I won't get my Erasmus scholarship.'

The plot was thickening. First the time screw, now the grade twist. My arm was beginning to hurt a little. I stole another glance at the lovely, brown Mediterranean eyes, now going slightly moist. Water – their natural element. A people of the waters. Seafarers, discoverers, conquerors, Christians, founders of empires. Like Erasmus' people.

'Please, sir!' she pleaded, as a big tear wobbled around in her eye, the bubble of the spirit level making rough ways plain. I was weakening fast.

'Miss Barroso,' I said – having, of course, already decided in her favour – 'the days, I'm afraid, of colonialism are over. Cultural hegemony is passé. Your Professor back in Lisbon will have to accommodate himself to the requirements of foreign educational establishments.'

She hardly understood, but victory was hers anyway. Sadistic dramatics, intellectual intimidation – the watery consolations of mean academics. The student, of course, is the innocent victim.

I looked steadily into her liquid eyes. No student is fully innocent either.

'Miss Barroso,' I said, 'it's like this. I really have an immense amount of work on my plate. But you seem to be in a particularly difficult situation. I'll do my best. If I can, I'll try and have your paper corrected and your certificate ready by Friday. But there's no guarantee, remember that, no guarantee! Come to me on Friday at 9 am.'

'Oh, sir…' she began.

'Do you believe?' I interrupted.

'Of course I believe you,' she replied.

'No,' I said, 'what I mean is, are you a Christian?'

'Yes, I am.'

'Do you pray?'

'Sometimes.'

'Well my advice to you is to pray as hard as you can for the next two days. More things are wrought by prayer, you

138

know!'

Hypocrite! Hardly a case in point!

'Oh I will, sir,' she said very earnestly. 'I will pray.'

'Friday at 9, then.'

When she left I looked at the *Pentecost* print, with the dove and the tongues of fire descending. She'll pray, and her prayers will be heard. What harm is there in a little bit of conniving, for Christ's sake?

She was at my door on the dot of nine. I handed her her certificate, without a word. I could see, I thought, that she had to restrain herself from embracing me. A question formed in my mind: 'Did you pray?' But I lost it somehow and instead I asked her,

'What's the word for 'goose' in your mother tongue?'

'For what?'

'Goose.'

'Ganso,' she said. 'Why?'

'Well,' I said, 'when you get back to Lisbon tell your Professor I said he was a proper ganso.'

'Oh I will, sir, I will tell him,' she said very earnestly.

Almost too earnestly.

'I suppose I'd better continue correcting these papers,' I said to myself. 'But first I'll have a cup of coffee and a look at the newspaper.'

*　　*　　*

High in the blue sky over the Alps, Elsa Barroso was feeling very happy. Another fifty minutes and she would be back home in Lisbon. She had her certificate in her case. She had got a good grade and her Erasmus scholarship was guaranteed. So her friends back at the university were right. They told her he would fall for the tear in her southern eyes. Silly old gander. And did he really believe she prayed?

139

HERO OF THE WEST

Matty Mulchrone was a nobody, really. He was wafted by a gentle, westerly breeze onto a small farm in west Mayo at some unrecorded time in the past. There were two donkeys on the farm, then came Matty, and then one of the donkeys had a foal. Days came over the land and fell across Matty and the donkeys, and nights came in from the Atlantic and fell on them, too. 'It's time to be going now,' someone told Matty when the two old donkeys died. So Matty mounted the foal and struck off down the lane, begod.

Later, quite some time later, the foal stopped to relieve himself, so Matty got off, too, and went over to the hedge. The foal finished first, saw his chance, took to his heels and sped away back to the distant grasses of west Mayo. A thorn in the hedge pricked Matty so he buttoned up and shifted off down the hill in the direction of the next hill. At the bottom he sat.

'Hop in,' said the curate, and Matty had been taken up and down seven more hills when the curate said: 'Your future is in Latin and Greek!' So they gave him a red Greek grammar and a blue Latin grammar and put him in the front seat in college. They decline his name 'Mulchrone, Mulchrousa, Mulchronn' and they set him in the back seat while Caesar was in Gaul. Once he was late for prayers because he didn't hear the bell. 'You'll be out on your ear, do you hear?' announced the deaf college President, and he was, by the next Angelus. 'Arise, my love, we'll go to Paris,' said the sergeant's daughter from down town. She took him to Dublin and put him on the next plane to Gaul. 'Matty, I'll join you when the thorn is out,' she whispered, and her warm tears moistened Erin's green sod as the Rolls Royce roar jetted Matty away.

Matty Mulchrone from west Mayo stood at the top of Avenue Hoche. His mouth open, he was wearing a red and green shirt, and three strands of the grey donkey's hair were still hidden in the folds of his trousers. He was slightly bent. It was then that another woman walked into his life: a vestal from Mayo who had been living in Paris for 27 years and spoke French with a Kiltimagh accent. They called her Petty Pou. More important, she was a great symbolist nun. She circled Matty clockwise, taking in the colour scheme; her eye shot, on the re-circle, down the right leg of the trousers to the hairs; the third time round she pressed a finger ever so lightly against Matty's shoulder and nodded when he winced. 'The perfect man,' she said to herself, 'at last he's here.' With a purity of vision which only long years of ascetic practice, close study of the symbolist tradition, and heroic perseverance in speaking French badly can have as their reward, this woman was given to understand the encounter in a way in which it is given to few to understand such things. 'A man to a fault,' she whispered, 'a man to a fault. Quick, Matty,' she said. 'You're young, I'm getting old. Be in time if you can. Hurry up!' Matty, outmanoeuvred by the ass, declined and defined, outclassed in the classics and expelled for being late, was taken by a firm hand and whisked unwillingly, with a slither and a stumble and inarticulate mumbles, into the convent and down the long, long corridor, over the waxy floor and slippery boards of Fontainbleau pinewood, on past medieval reverend mothers, holy tapestries, silver milk jugs in silent cabinets, remnants of hymns, alleluias trapped in inaccessible cobwebs, escaped love-sighs woven into silk curtains.

Forward, forward she drew him with her, with bated breath, unabated pace, while lumps of bog dirt rolled off his boots and his left fist tightened to a ball in his pocket. Her left hand tugged and melted in his right and he could not separate from her. Her fingers crept up inside his arm, along his veins, around his bones; they enveloped his brain, encircled his heart, entwined his guts and fastened his legs together siamesically. 'Oh!' she said 'we must stop! We've gone too far!' She was red to the gills. She melted out of him, stood facing him, gave him a wink. 'Time, Matty' she said, 'time. You're out of time. Grow up, mature, we may never meet again.' Then she turned him around and faced him down the long, long corridor they had just come up. She closed her eyes, lifted his Arran gansey a little, and fiddled till she found his galluses. Solid, black, elastic. She pulled, standing back a little. Matty didn't budge. Good. She pulled harder. The buttons stretched, Matty strained. Budge he did not. Better. Unnunilly then she raised the vestal leg and planted her heel in the small of his back. She pulled harder than ever and let suddenly go. Back down the corridor Matty trajected, pea-shot, windlassed, sucked, pucked, whirling, bounding and finally backsiding round the last corner and out with a bump again into Avenue Hoche. At the bottom end.

He re-winced. His body's bent now a right angle, he sat there balancing on his bottom. Legs like sticks straight and apart, his members made cosines to the triumphal monument in front of him. At the Sorbonne's Mathematical Institute, Professor Ruby was crimson with anger.

'The cosine,' he said, 'is the sine of the complement of a given arc or angle. It's perfectly clear. If you don't grasp that, we can't go on.'

A student in red, coming home from the lecture, knelt

beside Matty to give him advice.

'The view,' she said, 'is unique. Pay it a complement. Say: 'Hi Arc, you're lovely!''

'That's not right,' said a Jew, who knew more about Leviticus than Pythagoras, 'no eyes for ease! Don't be cheap!'

Matty's back was straight, his arms folded on his chest. A passing concierge noticed his missing hypotenuse.

'Get up off ... Get up off your ...' His voice quivered with upset. 'You're a mathematical lout!'

A crowd was gathering now. Another voice asked,

'Hard or soft?'

A maid made her way to the centre.

'Joan, that's me. And it's hard. By God, it's hard. It was always hard, for me.'

Still another voice, small and wet and away on a hill in Armenia, joined in:

'Soft? Ah, no. Ah, no, not at all. By Genesis, no, ah! It's hard. Always was and always will be. By my boat, it's hard!'

Who can pronounce the end of the dilemma? Soft or hard?

Paddy the punter, over from London for the gee-gees and the grand pricks, left his s's behind on Soho Square.

'Oho, it's quare, so it is. A prize,' he said, 'for whoever solves the conundrum of the Arc. The curate from Ars has his hand up, I see. Well, Curé, 've y'any idea which's right?'

'Soft, of course,' said the Abbé.

Then the monument itself pronounced its answer triumphantly:

'Hard, and that's it. After all, I should know!'

But a clochard from Kilalla stepped swaggering in.

'Jasus Christ Almighty, what are ye on about? It's always been soft and let no bloody Frog try and teach me

143

me own language.'

He spread a fierce glare around on the crowd and French resistance vanished. The coast was suddenly clear.

'Get up off it now anyway,' said the redeemer, 'and skidaddle. You're a disgrace to your country!'

He faced Matty in the direction of the nearest Metro station and his final words were:

'I won't be around to save you twice. Don't ever strike postures in France again, sitting or standing. And never come back till you've reached mathematical maturity. There's a side to you the French can't see and that's something they don't like. When their monuments talk, don't answer. It's absurd, do you hear? If you have roots, go now and look for them. If you haven't, put some down!'

Petty Pou, peeping round a silk curtain, sighed at the sight of Matty's fine red head sliding away slowly down the steps of the Metro. Matty went underground.

The station was Trocadero and the next station was Rue de la Pompe. The tube glided in and stopped abruptly. When the automatic door opened, Matty's left leg, de-siamesed again, lifted itself safely inside while his right one had to wait its turn. The beck came from the brain, but the train couldn't wait. Reflexing fast, the right leg betook itself to its mate, but the broad folds of the worsted trousers from the Foxford mills stuck fast in the door. A gentle young miss of thirteen spotted Matty's predicament. She gave her bag of grapes and her baguette to her granny to hold and then knelt to the task, tugging and pulling. 'His leg,' she thought 'is long and lovely, but how baggy are his britches!' She tugged and tugged, and pulled and pulled, and between one tremendous tug and one despairing pull the door opened automatically again, at la Pompe. Crowds swept out, sweeping Matty with them. 'That beautiful leg,' said the mademoiselle, 'is mine; I'll never let it go!' Leaving her granny, her grapes and her bread behind her, she followed the limb at its every stride.

Up the metro steps it went again, the beloved leg in the baggy trousers. Sharing each step with its brother leg, it moved Matty along a street, away from the centre, out towards the south. And the miss followed tenaciously, never letting it out of her sight. At the periphery she risked a quick look back at the city she thought she was leaving forever. Montmartre gleamed and Eifel's Tower was still standing. Her granny was half way up, desperately waving the baguette. 'Tower of Ivory,' prayed the miss, 'grant that I may always remain true to this leg.'

With every step that Matty took southwards the mademoiselle's excitement rose. She followed him close on the A 20. She kept peeping at the beau's limb as it went along. 'Mon chou' she said to it at Versailles, 'chouchou' she apostrophised it at Orleans, waving to Joan as they passed. But south of Limoges a juggernaut brushed them by and took the toes of the leg away. Mademoiselle clutched the mutilated member. She pulled off the boot and washed the wound with her tears at junction 33. Around that perfect but now-mauled leg she spun a long, white bandage of the purest love that trailed back to her days as a happy gurgling baby, to delightful oysters sucked with her granny, to the sweet-sad kiss she gave her puppy the day he died at the wheel of a bicycle. Around and around she wove the protective lint until her very eye, concentrating, cocooned itself around the pupa leg and the whole Matty mass began to whirl like tumbleweed at hurricane speed to the south, her grip on the leg tightening at every whirl. At Toulouse it broke off and spun away to the west. Still holding on, mademoiselle spun with it, bounding over Pau and Bayonne to touch down again at windy Biarritz. There the pupa matured into a beetle, and the lovelorn miss had to set out on the infinitely long and lonely road back to Paris, walking the insect on a leash of lost love lashed to her broken heart. The remains of Matty, meanwhile, spun eastwards, bounded off Narbonne and Nimes, and touched down on the front lawn of the papal palace in Avignon, where he toppled over and lay, a sorry exile.

A timely arrival, as it transpired. Exiled, rootless, confounded in Paris, undone by love on the roads, Matty rested there, undiscovered for the present, while within the palace in lustrous sateen robes sate at his diptych of polished oak His Holiness Pope John XXII of the golden nib, his serviceable quill now at rest beside a parchment on which the ink was still wet. Recollecting with little remorse and much comfort his suppression of the Templars, he had flung himself into the fray once more, relishing the certainty, based on divine inspiration, scriptural authority and an impeccable Latin style, that the papacy would prevail, what if the intractable natures of a Louis in Bavaria or a Frederick in Austria were impressing themselves with no little success on the heretical Visconti in Italy, what if the poverty zealots of the Franciscan Spirituals were proving embarrassing witnesses to the fatal opulence of his respected predecessors, if not of himself. He quaffed off the dregs of his cup of mead, which provided even greater warmth to his conviction that the bull he had just completed was of consummate importance for the faith, despite the futility of all his previous ones. Still, doubts gnawed. Had he not decided to remain in France but remove to Rome where the previous pontiffs were wont to reside; or had he resolved to practise the law in Paris, teach on in Toulouse, and prosecute the governance of Naples; nay had he determined in his youth to devote his talents to St. Thomas, patron of cobblers, and pursue the bootmaker's trade of his father; peradventure he might never have encountered those perfidious Britons who had arrived on a tandem from Albion to sow discord and sedition in his spiritual kingdom, and whose pounding

146

on the iron door of their prison cells below had but yester-night contrived to deprive him of a good night's sleep and provoke in him a gallous humour today. For what man, be he Pope or pauper, saint or scoundrel, can rise with composure and dignity on the morn that is morrow to a night of slamming and banging, utterly hostile to the comfort of Somnus' kisses? He rose, and resorting, before finally subscribing the new edict, to his adjacent supping room for further sustenance from his favoured pre-prandial beverage – such as the wisest of anointed sovereigns, in moments of great stress or distress, have ever found to be conducive to placidity of disposition and excellence of rhetoric (those handmaids of prudent politics and tolerant traditions), but, alack, also, through their alco-holic proportions, promotive of those inferior sentiments which somewhiles reside in inglorious vicinage to contentiousness and virulence and prove progenitive of conflicts, controversies, and contrarieties – His Holiness siffled thereof, paused, and pondering profoundly returned to his desk in the other room. He perused his text once more. A scholar and conscientious, he would check his sources. Groping in the dark recesses of the holy vestures in which he was arrayed, he fetched forth from an arcane pocket of noble nun's stitch, his mobile. With some timorousness he dialled the hotline number which he had already had reason to dial on more than one occasion while composing his edicts. Matthew himself answered.

'Pray, Your Sanctity, this is Papa Giovanni speaking.'

[- - -]

'No, the Twenty-Second.'

[- - -]

'That's right. But this is a new one. It is entitled *Sancta Romana et Universa Ecclesia*.'

[- - -]

'Yes, I know you don't have much time up there, but

147

there's just once reference I'd like to cross-check.'

[- - -]

'No, no. The Revised Standard Version.'

[- - -]

'Okay, I'll make it short. In Ch.16, v.18, did you write 'Thou art Peter and upon this rock I will build my church' or 'Thou art Petra and upon this rock I will build my church'?'

[- - -]

'Thanks a lot. I thought so. I just wanted to make sure – in case somebody like that reckless Franciscan below comes along some fine day and wants to instal 'Her Holiness' on my cathedra. Imagine! Tell Peter keep an eye out for Ockham when he comes a-knocking. See you.'

'Seems in bad sorts today,' said the Papa to himself, switching off his mobile and returning it to the secret depths of his canonicals.

His Holiness finally attached his signature with a flourish to his new edict, sealed it with his bull, and called aloud for John, his newly-employed servant, to come, whose defection from his quondam patron, Thomas of England, O.P., was imputable rather to the cold and rusty Avignon chains he saw depending from the thin white ankles of his incarcerated Dominican master, than, as the Pope erroneously opined, to the bedrock orthodoxy of his theological convictions.

Enter John on uncertain, bespatted feet, sleepy-eyed, bell-deaf, bearded and bent, balancing precariously on flabby labia the butt-end of a Gitanes that emitted white smoke through browned dentals. The declination of his attempted curtsey to his new master brought him perilously close to the mortification of a complete hori-zontality.

'Brother John,' said the Pope, 'it is my pleasure that your two fellow countrymen, who both of them have

148

strayed so far from the paths of righteousness that they durst contradict my divine teachings and stain the purity of our holy religion with perverse theses, should physic their sick souls with acts of penance and contrition. Wherefore this bull, John, is to serve as chief source of their spiritual enlightenment and instrument of their moral regeneration – and that of the great holy, Roman and universal Church, in addition. With yonder stylus and wax,' he said, indicating the diptych, 'they will each for penance write out this bull 500 times and subsequently disseminate it in every diocese under my sceptre. Bestir thee hence to the dungeons below, call out 'William of Ockham, OFM, and Thomas of England, OP' and command them to attend my pleasure here forthwith.'

From the ring of iron keys pendant from his leathern waistband he then undid the prison clavis.

'Lead them hither, and betimes!' he said, pressing the key into the bloodless hand of his seemingly faithful servant.

Wheezing, weak, re-enter John some short time later, alone, his breath uncertain, his eyes to the ground, a cold film of suspicion on the hand that effectuated the return of the key.

'They're gone!' wheezed John.

'Who? Whither?' said the Pope.

'Tom and Bill. Gone over the hill!'

'And my bull?'

John shrugged his shoulders, turned sleepily around and shuffled sheepishly out.

Alarums within and without. Bells ring. Bugles blare. Guards at their posts redouble their vigilance. Bridgeheads are blocked, fishermen's boats commandeered, homing pigeons alerted, eagles deployed on rooftops, all post-roads placed under surveillance, long-distance runners engaged for the chase. The whole city is roused for the hunt. Find the fugitives. Apprehend the renegades. Deliver the dastards to justice.

His mobile was ringing a long time before His Holiness finally heard it.

'John here.'

[- - -]

'Sorry, but it's so loud here at the moment – pure bedlam. I can't hear my own ears.'

[- - -]

'Vessel of clay? A worm and no man? On the lawn? I don't get it!'

[- - -]

'Your namesake! I see, kind of. Well, if the Boss says so …'

[- - -]

'See you.'

He switched off his phone, meditated for a moment, shook his head. Then taking the sealed edict from the desk, he placed it in a capacious side-pocket of his ample robes and called once more for John. John returned.

'My good and faithful servant' said the Pope, 'a divine afflatus has come upon me. My bull is now to be put in an earthenware pot, fed to a worm on the lawn, entrusted to a creature made of clay. Who can fathom the depths of divine revelation, who can comprehend the ways of the Lord? Let us take with us a spade and go into the garden.'

Arrived on the lawn, it was Brother John who first spotted, among the terracotta cisterns, potsherds, earthenware amphorae and terra sigillata bowls from nearby La Gramfesenque that lay scattered around in disarray, the prostrate vessel of clay. 'Look,' said John, 'look there!' The Pope looked. Then, nose on finger, he pondered the predicament, prayed for guidance and enlightenment, and, benefitting from a high-voltage flash of inspiration, finally succeeded in aligning the Evangelist's cryptic communiqué with his own scriptural erudition and the principles of pure logic to recognize in Matty Mulchrone from Mulranny the creature made of clay divinely pre-destined to disseminate his bull.

'John,' said His Holiness, 'repair post-haste to the coachhouse and bring hither the paints, the brushes, the yellow maillot, the template and the tandem.'

John returned, dejected.

'I couldn't find a Templar.'

'Nincompoop!' blustered forth the Vicar of Christ, momentarily failing on the dignity required of his sacred office. But then:

'Brother John, those knights, you should know, have been suppressed and do no more exist. Go find me the *template*.'

The spring in the step of the returning servant spelt success. At His Holiness' behest, John then extended upon a clearing in the shrubs the yellow vest of finest lawn, and placed thereon the template. Whereafter he knelt stiffly down and with brush poised between bony fingers attended further papal directives.

'S. R. U. E.,' said the media-conscious Pope. 'In bright red.'

That done, he awaited further instructions.

'Inflate the rear cycle wheel.'

That, too, done, the next injunction was a sign, no words. John comprehended, slowly, the aim: to make Matty more media-natty. They divested him of his native Arran pullover and dressed him in an alien maillot. They stripped him of his Foxford Mills trousers and manipulated him into a pair of blue jeans. Then they contrived, with no less prodigality of effort than limitation of ability, to raise him whom they had looked upon into a quasi-perpendicular position. S.R.U.E. shone candescent from his back, the yellow-and-blue colour scheme accommodating national sentiments: the investiture was a success. Next His Holiness requested of his servant a Gitanes and a match. But the image of a Pope smoking a Gitanes proved too iconoclastic for John's untutored imagination, the fabric of which had already been stretched to ripping point by the unexpected appearance of a mutilated Irishman among pots and vases on the lawn in Avignon, so he fainted at Matty's foot. The Pontiff availed himself of this providential opportunity and removed a match from the tinder-box of his momentarily insensible servant, and a cigarette from his ashy, hold-all cowl. With that, Brother John began to stir again, as if the circumstance of a smoking and a pilfering Pope shook so the single state of his moral being that consciousness needs must return to know if such an outrage was true or no. Then he heard the Pontiff say to Matty:

'Matthew, Matthew, your namesake in heaven hath revealed your advent to me. Arduous was your coming hither, unexpected your arrival, precipitous your fall but glorious your destiny. I herewith appoint you my evangelising angel of truth. Go forth unto all the nations, but first to the Romans, and proclaim on this your cycle that salvation comes, no matter what road one takes, through the Holy Roman and Universal Church. Arrived in Rome, you shall light this cigarette, whose smoke will be as a signal alike to believer and atheist, convert and heathen, that when the Pope resides in France the faith is fearless and free.'

So saying, he inserted the match and the cigarette in Matty's hip pocket, and attached the bull firmly with string to the carrier of the tandem. Then he beckoned to John to assist him in mounting Matty thereon. It proved a difficult task to find a balance, what with the vacuity within the right trouser leg, saddle springs dangerously askew and, in combination with the thorn, utterly inimical to progeny, a buckled front wheel, and air escaping imperceptibly from the back one. 'Amen, Amen, Amen,' were the only words that carried on John's weak and wheezing breath, as with left hand on saddle and right hand on Matty's back he helped on the east side push the peirastic peddler of redemption waveringly over the lawn, the Pope pushing with equal strain on the west side, right hand on saddle and left hand on back. No vento wheels, no aluminium tubes, no monocoque carbon fork, no bottle holder or hydration pack, no odometer for Matty, as his tandem is faced towards the eternal city. At their approach to the main exit of the palace courtyard, the great wooden gates opened, and now the din and pandemonium and cheers of the roused masses, congregated on the squares and thorough-fares and along the banks of the river, rolled over them like a tidal wave. They made their way slowly towards the bridge, the crowds waving banners, strewing palms, shooting photos, raising their arms and holding small children aloft on their shoulders. Suddenly a file of motor-cyclists, some equipped with TV cameras, appeared at the far end of the street, blowing their horns and swerving rhythmically from side to side to prevent the multitudes from encroaching too far onto the roadway. Then a high-pitched, whirring ululation was heard, a tang of rubbery attrition was carried on the warm breeze, a small Japanese tourist raised his excited son, ululating too with joy, on his shoulders, a de-frocked Irish priest, outmanoeuvring the wardens, sprinted naked across to the other side, and then there they were, all 198 of them in fast approach, Stephen Roche leading the Tour. Utterly oblivious, the Pope and his auxiliary ushered wobbling Matty unsteadily on his tandem straight across the road, in the path of the speeding athletes, towards the bridgehead. Roche, seeing the yellow jersey with his initials on it (and those of the Union Europeanne) in bright red colours, believed he was afflicted with double vision and collapsed over his fork, bringing the rest of the field tumbling down on top of him. The cameras and crowds switched their interest to Matty and his pushers as they reached the crest of the bridge of Avignon. The tourists, tourers (revived again) and cheering throngs crowded behind them onto the straining wooden structure to witness Matty's historic departure. With one almighty effort and a final heave-ho, John and John propelled Matty down the bridge's slight incline, over the Rhone, into the Holy Roman Empire of the German Nation, and on towards Rome to spread the word of truth throughout the world. Then the bridge began to oscillate perilously and the Pontiff lost his cool for the second time that day. 'Get back quickly off the bridge, you asses!' he roared, as 18 of its 22 arches went crashing into the river below. 'I must have that fixed,' said the pontifex maximus to John, as they trundled back through the throbbing city to the peace of the papal palace and to vespers.

Proselytized, re-designed, re-routed, Matty is now commissioned on a long, lone pilgrimage for the church militant, set in perpetual motion by a Johannine push that now carried him forward at a constant, unchanging pace on his one-speed, God-sped, crock of a bicycle. Impermeable to rain or rainbow, river or rapid – impervious to perfume or stench, gas or vapour – resistant to pot-hole and puncture, avalanche and earthquake – immune to hernia and haemorrhoids, heathenism and heresy – undeterred by dog or dragon, daylight or darkness – breaking barriers, records and wind – he appeared sporadically on radar screens as a speck of dust, on TV-screens as a star, on hospital screens as an unknown virus.

Pilgrimaging east on his one-pedal tandem, Matty now passed over delectable mountains, through valleys of tears and vanity fairs, beside meadows of cheer and sloughs of despondence, through villages of virtue and cities of vice.

He was observed and ignored, cheered on and jeered at, ridiculed by burghers as a country clodhopper, worshipped as a hero by the handicapped, anathematized by theologians as a wheeler-dealer of bull-shit. He was an enigma to sportsmen, a puzzle to historians, a phenomenon to philosophers, a sensation to the media, an embarrassment to fashion designers and a mere nonentity to politicians, stock-exchange gurus and all-powerful company executives.

One such executive-director was the 6ft. 10 in. and 152 kg. A. J. F. Goodbody-Chainey. Rather than give the company he founded his own unwieldy name, he simply called it 'Giant', reflecting his own massive physique and the hoped-for dimensions of his bicycle company's future development. Depressed by the after-the-news business report showing a five-days-in-a-row plummeting of share prices, he sat upright and uncomfortable and sighed deeply in his carved Chippendale chair with the fanciful spandrels. The board meeting the next day, called to discuss the worst crisis in the company's history, would be no easy ride. He was about to switch off and zap over to the sports channel when a news flash showed messenger Matty now rimming it over the narrow cobblestone streets of the old city of Nice, no air at all left in his back tyre. Luckily Mr. A. J. F. Goodbody-Chainey was video-recording the programme. He played it back. The tandem struck him. He played it back again. Who was the cyclist? Where was he going? He rang the TV station and got more information. Then an idea came into his mind, a very good idea, in fact a brilliant idea the more he thought about it. He sat up all night and worked on it, making diagrams, drawing sketches, preparing transparencies, burning CDs and midnight oil. When he strode into the Giant Bicycle Corporation's meeting the next morning with a heavy brief-case in his hand and a flip-chart under his arm, he exuded an air of confidence and composure normally incompatible with a sleepless night and out of kilter with the depressed state of the stock market. Awaiting him with long, pale faces at the round, mahogany conference table with its four stout legs were the CEO, the Company Chairman, the Advertising Manager and the Financial Director. Hardly had the minutes of the previous meeting been taken as read when, lighting his cigar, the Director fused the electric atmosphere with 'Well, then gentlemen!' and sparked off a cloudburst of reproaches and recriminations. The CEO accused the Financial Director of employing company resources to feed white elephants, the Financial Director accused the Advertising Manager of shepherding a whole flock of lame ducks, the Advertising Manager told the Company Chairman that in matters of sales techniques and media effectiveness he was the original bull in a china shop, and the Company Chairman said the CEO deserved an Oscar for mismanagement. Hot and fat under his tight collar, the undersized CEO finally stood up to command attention and launched into a common tirade against the other three, glancing from time to time towards Mr. A. J. F. Goodbody-Chainey for approval. He concluded his philippic with waning acrimony and waxing bombast:

'The state of our company's health, respected colleagues, is not calamitous, it is carcinomatous. Our hitherto reliable blue chip segment is nothing now but the laughing-stock of the exchange. Up to recently, our Revenue Per Partner figures were the envy of our competitors and an enigma to analysts of the Purchasing Managers' Index. This present slump will, if we are not prepared to buck the trend with the horns of economic acuity and advertising acumen, scuttle prospective takeovers, jeopardize the goodwill of investment banks, alienate our franchised dealers and send the cycling community scurrying off-road. We must re-think, we must update, we must innovate, we must go global!'

He sat down, and now the Director took over. He stood up, and up, till he reached his full height. Stern, intimidating, determined but calm, he said:

'Gentlemen, I shall not detain you with many words. My unreserved support goes to the CEO. If radical, and successful, changes are not implemented in this company forthwith, then it will be the mountain bike instead of the Audi for you two' (to the Chairman and the CEO) 'and you two' (to the Financial Director and the Advertising Manager) 'can wear your butts off on a tandem till there is a notable hike in share prices.' Then looking gravely but quizzically at each of them individually, he said. 'There is one question I'd like to put to you, sirs. Ponder well before you answer. The question is this: 'What, in your opinions, is the most important thing in a modern, successful business company?' I'll give you two minutes to think.'

They thought. The four answers they came up with were: Diversification, E-Marketing, Strategic Planning, Motivational Incentives.

'No, no, no and no,' said Mr. Goodbody-Chainey. 'No wonder our bicycles sales are racing downhill! The clue to all successful entrepreneurship, the basic quality required of the soul of every single employee from the owner to the fired workman, the principle that governs the whole evolutional progress of combine, concern and corporation, is Imagination. Just imagine! Let me give you an example of what I mean.'

He walked around the table, set up his flip-chart, opened the TV-press, took his video and his CDs from his brief case, plugged in the overhead projector, laid out his transparencies in a neat row, let down the automatic blinds, switched off the lights, and launched on his power-point presentation. First he showed his recording of the news flash, then Matty's progress – first at normal speed, then in slow motion, then backwards, and then close up. This he followed with an impressive series of simple diagrams in bright colours, showing every part of the cycle and the cyclist. With his laser pointer he focused attention on the saddle, the bell, the tyres, the frame, the carrier, the papal bull, the shirt, the shoes, the semi-occupied jeans, the cigarette sticking up out of Matty's hip pocket.

'Now,' he said, switching on the lights again and addressing the other members of the board, 'to the dull and the mundane what I have shown you is totally common-place, tiresomely trivial and of absolutely no significance. Just a handicapped cyclist on his way into town. The truth of the matter, however, is that what we have before us constitutes the most extraordinary advertising chip of all time. All you need is a little imagination to see that this represents the greatest sales potential this galaxy has ever witnessed. Can any of you tell me why?'

A haze of confusion and bewilderment settled in the eyes and descended on the minds of the company's big brass. There was no answer at all. "I'll give you two minutes to think!" Again they thought. This time they drew a complete blank.

'I'll help you a little,' said the disappointed but chivalrous company founder. 'If we could get the exclusive rights to that unique bicycle and that unique cyclist, we could use every single element of it as an advertising platform. The world's leading institutes, agencies, businesses, consortiums and syndicates would come on their bended knees begging for the privilege of investing their millions in one or other simple bicycle part. For example –'

He switched off the lights again, and directing his pointer to the chain of Matty's cycle, he observed:

'I don't have to tell you what that is. Now try and

158

imagine the significance this part would have for international hotel groups, fast-food providers and anti-smoking campaigners wanting to advertise. How we could capitalize on that!'

But he identified a certain degree of mesmerization in his listeners.

'Gentlemen, it is clear to me that you are still in the dark about this new concept; it has taken you completely by surprise. You will need, I see, a little time to reflect – I myself have spent the whole night, I confess, working out with infinite care and imaginative finesse the in se unimaginable social, historical and, above all, economic implications of this phenomenon. I would ask you to work through these handouts, examine the diagrams, do the exercise at the end by subjecting it to the intensest possible rays of your imaginations, and we shall meet again at 11 o'clock. We have no time to lose. Imagination is money. We are about to take one huge step into the golden age of our bicycle company.'

He strode out and left them there, brainstorming.

The exercise was a simple one of linking. On the left there was a list of cycle and cyclist parts, and on the right a corresponding list of possible investors. The task was:

Link the (lettered) parts on the left with the appropriate (numbered) organizations on the right, and (be prepared to) give an explanation of your selected links:

Cycle and cyclist parts   Potential investors
(a) saddle   (1) jockey clubs
(b) springs   (2) mineral water companies
(c) chain   (3) anti-smoking
                                campaigners/fast-fooders
(d) bar   (4) chambers of barristers/pub-
                                owners associations

(e) carrier

(f) tyres

(g) frame

(h) ball-bearings

(i) semi-occupied

(j) bell

(k) pedals

(l) shirt and shoes

(m) papal bull

(n) spokes

(o) fork

(p) leg

(5) forwarding agents

(6) finance ministries (inflation control dept.)

(7) mafia

(8) genetic engineering laboratories

(9) paraplegic olympics trouserscommittees

(10) church organizations

(11) drug dealers

(12) sports outfitters

(13) Red Bull

(14) press and politics PR

(15) agricultural co-ops

(16) UEFA

Add your own ideas here:

....
....
....
....

Back on the dot at 11, Mr. A. J. F. Goodbody-Chainey could see at a glance the transformation that had taken place in his board members. A quick check showed him they had worked out all the 16 links correctly. Their enthusiasm now knew no bounds, though they produced no new ideas of their own. 'First,' said the Director 'we must secure the exclusive marketing rights to Matty. That's your job,' he said to the Advertising Manager and the latter grabbed his mobile from off the table, ran helter-skelter to his Audi and zoomed off towards Nice, blinding low-flying doves and high-flying hawks with the dust he raised as he raced across the Alps. Of his own accord, the Financial Manager made a plunge for the desk phone and alerted his brokers on Wall Street and Paternoster Square, urging them to contact immediately international investment agencies, dollar-shaking sheiks, money-lenders and money launderers. The CEO took down all the customer and product files from the shelves and piled them up on his desk for scrutiny. The Chairman went surfing the Internet to google out the most important embassy, consular and chamber-of-commerce addresses from China to Chile. The Director decided he would himself make the first direct contact, so he rang his old Red Bull friend in Salzburg, Mr. Dietrich Mateschitz.

'Don't you remember me, Didi? We met in a shop in China in the late 80ies when you got that great Red Bull idea from your communist friends.'

[- - -]

'Yes, that's me. You did well to remember the name! But just call me Tony, please.'

[- - -]

'No, no, I soon saw that it was not commercially effective so I changed it to the Giant Bicycle Corporation.'

[- - -]

'No, I'm afraid not. They had too many bicycles already. Coals to Newcastle, you know.'

[- - -]

'Downhill, unfortunately. But listen, I've got a wonderful new idea. That's why I'm ringing you – I'm sure you'll be just as excited as I am when I tell you about it. You see, there's a funny Irish guy with one leg moving along the Mediterranean coast on a tandem, with a papal bull behind him, on the road, I've been told, to Rome.'

[- - -]

'Of course they do, but this one could also be the one that leads our company into a glorious future. And that's where your soft drinks come in.'

The one company founder then explained to the other

company founder his vision for the future of both companies based on the infinite advertising potential latent in Matty and his bike. And, to boot, there were a priori elements of similarity and correspondence between the cycle-cyclist (his name, the document), on the one hand, and the soft-drinks inventor (his name, the product) on the other, that were nothing short of portentous and susceptible only of one interpretation: divine predestination.

'Nomen est omen,' said Mr. A. J. F.

[- - -]

'Yes, yes, you're right. In very bad taste indeed. That part of your name we would, of course, ignore. But don't you think it a splendid idea, a unique advertising opportunity?'

[- - -]

'Excellent. Excellent. I thought you would. In the meantime I shall work out a portfolio and bring it with me. In Monte Carlo, then, after the race. And by the way, all the best for your team!'

That was a good start. Hardly had A. J. F. (Tony) Goodbody-Chaney put down the phone when it rang again. A very flustered Advertising Manager was at the other end.

'Sorry to have to report bad news, sir, but this Mr. Matty is proving a very hard nut to crack. I drove up behind him, beside him, in front of him – he didn't even seem to see me! I blew my horn at him, flashed my lights, even touched his back wheel with my bumper, but the reaction was nil. I held a microphone to his mouth, asked him who was his agent, did he have sponsors, what the letters meant on the back of his shirt – but not a word. I begged him for a very short interview – not a word. Maybe he's deaf. Maybe he's blind. Maybe he has a magnetic membrane in his nose, guiding him unerringly on to Rome like a homing pigeon. I brought the Audi to a sudden standstill right in front of him, but he just rode up the back and down the front and continued on his way. I stalked him for miles, but at times I lost track of him altogether when he rode along railway tracks, through dark tunnels, under waterfalls or over mountain ridges. As a matter of fact, he has just come into earshot again: I can hear him now, scraping along the gravel path between the tombstones of the local graveyard. There is no air in his tyres, his saddle is totally awry, and his front wheel is as buckled as a ram's horn. What, sir, am I to do?'

Mr. A. J. F., in contrast to his voluble Advertising Manager, was brief. He informed him that Mateschitz was nibbling, a meeting had been planned after the formula 1 race, and if all went well for the Red Bull team, the prospects were very encouraging. He signed off by telling his Advertising Manager to stick close with Matty, not to let him out of his sight again: 'Follow him up to Monte Carlo!'

Still impelled by the papal push, Matty was now pedalling on for Monaco when a bent and hooded figure came into view, some 500 metres ahead. Trudging wearily along the grass edge of the road in the same direction as Matty, the now footsore Franciscan, William of Ockham, was heading in his worn-out sandals for Bavaria and for Louis. He prayed as he went along, reciting the Litany of the Saints in a meek and humble voice:

Sancte Johannes, ora pro nobis.
Sancte Thoma, ora pro nobis.
Sancte Jacobe, ora pro nobis.
Sancte Philippe, ora pro nobis.
Sancte Bartolomaee, ora pro nobis.
Sancte Matthaee, ora pro nobis.

But the clattering of the bike as Matty approached rang a little bell in his memory. It proved too great a distraction and, litania interrupta, he turned slowly around, only to see the impeccable tandem on which he and Thomas of England had triumphantly entered Avignon, and which that preposterous, latinate John XXII had confiscated, now being jockeyed along by a lone and unknown rider, the lovely vehicle reduced to a flat, rickety, buckled, bone-shaking velocipede. His heart, and feet, bled for his bike. Seized by a sudden, uncontrollable passion, he attempted to pull the rider off as he passed, but his weak endeavour had as little obstructional effect on Matty as the Advertising Manager's Audi. Then a flash of spiritual enlightenment, combining with a sudden weakness of the flesh, possessed him, and he hopped onto the vacant saddle behind Matty. Such was his gratitude to the Lord for this relief to his weary feet that his litany developed into a canticle, and in a lovely tenor voice he sang out to all the little birds and beasts that cared to listen to him:

Oro, the rattlin' bike,
Off to Monte Carlo – O,
Rare bike, rattlin' bike,
Off to Monte Carlo – O.

Wafted along on invisible papal power, the brown folds of his threadbare robes fluttered gently in the warm summer breeze. Ockham enjoyed the effortless progress he was now making as pillion to Matty. God had shown mercy to his humble, dutiful servant. Then his eye fell on the cigarette and the matchstick protruding from the front-man's hip pocket. In a spontaneous act of petty counter-pilfering, he put his long, slender fingers gingerly around the Gitanes and, placing his first-ever cigarette between his pure lips, he lit up. He closed his eyes and inhaled deeply, and when he exhaled again little rings of smoke swirled daintily like prayers from his Rosary beads up into the deep azure of the heavens. Rapt in a pleasure deeper than any that the contemplation of nature or the exquisite practices of asceticism had hitherto afforded him, he was prepared now to be towed on forever, an easy rider on the no longer rugged road to eternity. When the Sky News motorbike drove slowly by, the Franciscan bestowed a benign smile on the camera and a gentle wave of aromatic bonhomie on the camera-man.

When Mr. A. J. F. Goodbody-Chainey saw the news flash that evening, his customary composure gave way to incipient panic. Had the church once more got there first? Had the powerful tobacco lobby been the possessor of privileged information and taken unfair advantage of it? Was the chanson industry already trying to manipulate the charts for the forthcoming Eurovision Song Contest? He got on to his Advertising Manager at once, who assured his boss that he was keeping a very close watch on the situation, but could not make any prognosis at that point of time as to how things might develop because the determining circumstances were changing almost by the hour and were completely outside his control. When A. J. F. insisted that immediate action had to be taken, that an interview with Matty or something was a sine qua non, that his, the advertising manager's, job and jalopy were other-wise in jeopardy, the latter shrugged his shoulders at his mobile and pulled a long face – he loved his Audi.

'If he doesn't speak, maybe he can write,' pursued the Director of the Giant Bicycle Corporation. Has he any written documentation with him?'

[- - -]

'But the bull isn't his, is it! Is there anything else? Has he any letters on him? Any papers? Any records?'

[- - -]

'What about a pocket book. Or better still, a diary?'

[- - -]

'Then write one for him yourself, you dullard!' said A. J. F., losing patience.

He switched off.

These yuppies today, he mused, have the best education our modern system can offer, and pole-vaulting ambition as well, but they have no imagination. That's their great deficiency. Though he said it himself, that out-of-the-blue idea of ghost-writing a diary for Matty wasn't a bad one at all, actually. In fact it was quite brilliant, come to think of it. If they had a diarist for Matty, they could invent fictitious facts about his childhood, make startling revelations about his puberty, give a graphic account of the tragic accident that led to the loss of his right leg, delineate a mysterious chain of events leading to his personal intimacy with the Pope in exile, and, most importantly, dramatize the traumatic experience that gave rise to his eternal passion for the pedals. If well done, it would provide material for an epic film or a peak-time documentary series that at the same time would be an advertising campaign par excellent for Giant bicycles. Why, he asked himself, did he have to do all the imagining in his company.

He called the Company Secretary into his office, and with barely concealed pride outlined for him in glowing terms his next innovative idea for the redemption of the firm. His ardour slowly fanned a spark of interest in the Secretary, and when the boss insisted they needed a top-class ghost writer for Matty's diary as soon as possible, his imagination took flame and, after pondering for a few seconds, he came up with a super-duper suggestion as to how to go about getting a top-drawer script-writer.

'I'll get on to my old friend Gutemberg in Mainz. If it's not too late, maybe he could still place an ad in his revolutionary Bible. Just imagine, the first printed and unlimited edition of that great book containing our advertisement: 'Wanted immediately – Ghost-writer for diary of Very Important Person. Apply to the Giant Bicycle Corporation."

A. J. F. was pleased.

Gutemberg was most helpful, but regretted that everything had already been set up for the printing and no rearrangement of matrixes or plates was now possible. However, there was a fly-leaf in his incunabulum between the Old Testament and the New Testament, i.e. between Malachi and Matthew, and he could prepare a wooden block for a very short text, if that was any help.

'An optimal placement,' said the Company Secretary, and gave Gutemberg the go-ahead.

Gutemberg's Bible was a huge success.

The four applicants for the ghost-writer job were short-listed to three: a gentleman from England, a lady from Holland and a lady from Austria. (The fourth, who signed his/her letter of application, 'A Holy Spirit', was discarded as being spurious and irreverent and not of serious intent.) The three were called for an interview and appeared two days later before the Financial Director, the Company Chairman, the CEO and the Director. They made their individual entry according to age (youngest first) and in alphabetical, reverse chronological, and gender-correct order. A timid knock and then the high, oak door of the board room opened slowly. There entered with light footfall and downcast eyes a pale young girl with a slender volume in one hand. She stepped up unsteadily to her interviewers.

'Take a seat,' said the Chairman, surprised at her sex. 'I see you have signed yourself 'Frank' in your letter of application. We presumed that was your Christian name and were expecting ...'

'No, my family name. My first name is Anne. And I'm Jewish, not Christian. And I'm a girl.'

'Well, Miss Frank,' said the Chairman, 'why would a young Dutch girl like you be interested in ghost-writing a diary?'

'I'm not Dutch, I'm German!'

'That's not relevant at the moment. What, Miss, are your claims to fame as a diarist?'

'This,' she said, holding up the little slim volume. 'My own diary.'

'And what significance has your little German diary?'

'Not German, Dutch,' she said. 'It's written in Dutch.'

The Chairman began to tap loudly with his pen on the mahogany desk. Miss Frank felt that for some reason the interview was not going in her favour.

'How long is your diary?' asked the CEO with greater sang-froid.

'324 pages.'

'And its subject-matter?'

'Myself.'

Miss Frank seemed afraid to talk too much about her work.

'What period of time does your diary cover?'

'Two years and two months. From June 1942 to August 1944.'

The Director, seeing that the book in her hand was in English, asked her if she might not like to read a passage for them.

'We'd like to get to know your style a little.'

'Would you like the famous passage about my vagina getting wider all the time?'

'Please, spare us such details. Begin at the beginning. The opening passage is always the most important.'

She opened her diary at page one and started reading:

It's an odd idea for someone like me to keep a diary, not only because I have never done so before, but because it seems to me that neither I nor, for that matter, anyone else will be interested in the unbosomings of a thirteen-year-old schoolgirl ...

'Thank you, that will suffice,' said the Chairman, and

dismissed her rather peremptorily while asking her to send in the next candidate.

'And it was made into a film, too, and won the Pulitzer Prize,' added Miss Frank, as she gently closed the door behind her. She wasn't even sure if they heard her.

A few moments later the great oak door opened slowly a second time and there entered a small, friendly dog on his two hind legs. Pitting all his little canine strength against the unfair leash that was forcing him into that undignified posture, he fixed his cunning eye immediately on the round, stout legs of the mahogany table. Onto the other end of the leash was holding the veiny hand of a dim-sighted old lady, beautifully dressed in national costume, a white stick in her other hand, a kaleidoscopic corsage arranged in the bodice of her coatdress, and a plastic C&A bag on one arm. The chivalrous CEO bounded to her assistance and guided her to the chair, the excited little dog still nosily exploring as much of the new terrain as the leash's length permitted him to reconnoitre.

'Miss Anna Mozart…' began the Director, looking at the notes in front of him.

'Yes,' she said, 'that is who I am. I am from Austria. My full name is Maria Anna Wallpurga Ignatia Mozart. I am better known, however, as Nannerl'

'And do you mind my asking if you are …'

'You need not ask me. That question is one of two that have been put to me hundreds, nay thousands, of times already. It is the first question I am always asked at interviews or when people meet me on the street, and it is one which, if you will allow, is a great source of displeasure to me. The answer is, 'Yes, I am,' but I refuse to play second fiddle, as it were, to my more illustrious brother. He may have written music as a sow piddles, but I was the better musician. My father knew that, too, but he was much more interested in a career for his son that for his daughter, so I was compelled to take a back seat. It's always the same, isn't it? We women are second-class citizens as far as men are concerned. Will we ever gain equality? I wasn't even allowed to marry the man I loved, but was coerced by my father into a marriage of convenience with an old widowed fogey and lead a dog's life down the country.'

She gave an automatic reflex tug on the leash to Pimperl, who was suspiciously circling one of the befriended table-legs at that stage.

'But the bold Joannes Chrysostomus Wolfgangus Theophilus took to wife a flirtigig whom my father detested but still accepted. It's a man's world alright. In that regard, I should like to make an inquiry of you, sirs, if I may.'

She took her monocle from out her bodice and put it to her eye.

'What percentage of this interviewing committee is composed of women?'

'Our company produces just as many bicycles for women as for men, and your inquiry is not at all ad rem' replied the Company Secretary, non sequiturally.

'Perhaps we could continue the interview,' said the Director. 'The question I was going to ask you a few moments ago was, in fact, quite a different one. Do you happen to come from Salzburg in Austria? If you do, perhaps you know …'

She raised her hand, by way of interruption once more.

'Please, please,' she said. 'That's the second question that everybody asks. Well, the answer is, No, I don't. I never met him. And I haven't the least interest in soft drinks or Formula 1 racing. That's the kind of thing my brother would have loved.'

Slightly nettled, Mr. Chainey-Goodbody became more business-like.

'Might we have a list of your diary publications to

date?'

She fumbled in the C&A bag and brought forth a volume that was even more slender than that of the previous interviewee.

'What is its matter?'

'Family affairs. Visits and visitors. Games we played. Fashion. Pimperl's digestive problems. Papa's financial problems.'

'Number of pages?'

'136.'

'And what period of time does it cover?'

'Eight years, from May 1775 to September 1783.'

'Let me see. That's an average of 17 pages per year. Not as prolific as your brother I should think!'

Peeved, riled, stung once more by the odious comparison, she gave a 'let's go' tug to the leash just at the psychological moment when Pimperl's liason with the table-leg was reaching its urinary climax. The untimely interruption caused a misdirection of the dog's otherwise unerring aim, and the CEO's shiny shoe became the unintended and, for the moment, unnoticed target of Pimperl's micturation.

'Please, Miss Mozart, would you be so kind as to read us a little passage from your diary before you leave us?'

'Certainly not! First, my eyes are too weak for reading now. Secondly, I can see that as a woman I have no chance of getting the job in any case. Thirdly, I am of the considered opinion that you would not be in the least interested in the boring daily round of an 18th-century woman's life. And fourthly, you can read it yourselves at your leisure when I am gone.'

So saying, she rose with huffed dignity from the chair, placed her diary on the table, took up her white stick, and exerting emphatic pressure on the leash, ushered Pimperl and herself doorwards. The gallant CEO rose slowly to accompany them out but almost lost his balance as he slipped on the puddle at his feet. Then he noticed his tainted shoes. Had Nannerl overheard his expletives as she left, she might have roundly rated him as a hater of animals; she would surely, if involuntarily, have been reminded of her famous brother's sometimes salacious language.

The door opened for the third and last time and in stepped Samuel Pepys, Esq., the assurance of an Admiralty Secretary sitting upon him from sconce to sole. Sporting resplendent locks and a too russet tan that might have resulted from over-exposure to the sun-lamps of a solarium, he took his seat in front of the bicycle board. His observant eyes moved beneath singed eyebrows from one to the other of the interviewers, as if he was examining their physical state of health or the strength of their constitutions.

Mr. A. J. F. Goodbody-Chaney himself began the interview.

'I see from your letter of application, Mr. Pepys, that you have quite some experience in diary writing. Ten tomes is quite a respectable output. What extent of time do those volumes cover?'

'Approximately ten years, sir. From January 1st, 1660, to May 31st, 1669.'

'And what, pray, is the general substance of the work?'

'Life in London, the Great Fire, the Black Death.'

'I see. Very interesting, no doubt. Could you, perhaps, say something about your style of writing? Or, better, could you read a short passage for us?'

'I do not have a copy by me, sir. But, by your leave, I should be pleased to give a passage by rote.'

'Do so, then.'

'Coded or deciphered, sir?'

'Well, deciphered, I suppose.' The CEO nodded. 'Yes,

deciphered.'

'I shall begin at the beginning.'

Mr. Pepys stood up and declaimed in a fine Cambridge accent:

Jan. 1st. This morning (we living lately in the garret) I rose, put on my suit with great skirts, having not lately worn any other clothes but them. Went to Mr. Gunning's chapel at Exeter House, where he made a very good sermon upon these words: "That in the fulness of time God sent his Son, made of a woman," etc; showing that by "made under the law" is meant his circumcision, which is solemnized this day. Dined at home in the garret, where my wife dressed the remains of a turkey, and in the doing of it she burned her hand. I staid at home all the afternoon, looking over my accounts: then we went with my wife to my father's, and in going observed ...

'Thank you very much, Mr. Pepys,' said A. J. F. 'That will be enough for the moment. Could you wait outside for a short while.'

'Certainly, sirs,' said Pepys. 'But before I leave there's one little point of fact on which I should be delighted to receive some enlightenment.'

'Namely?'

'Who is the Very Important Person whose diary you advertised to be ghost-written?'

'That,' said the Director, 'you will be told if and when you are appointed to the post.'

Samuel Pepys, Esq., bowed and left.

The board members of the Giant Bicycle Corporation held a short post-interview conference. All four considered Miss Frank too diffident, too juvenile, too intimate, too fractious, too tight-lipped; all four saw Miss Mozart as being too domestic, too expansive, too touchy, too emanci-feminist, a chip-on-the-shoulder type; all four saw Mr. Pepys, by virtue of his publications to date, his harrowing

173

experiences, his command of language (the CEO set great store by this particular point) and his overall panache, as the obviously right man for the job. Mr. Pepys was called back into the board room, informed of his success, filled in on Matty, on the Director's vision of his future role in the expansion of the company, on the urgency of the matter and on the importance of picking up the trail before Matty or Mateschitz reached Monte Carlo. Delighted with the appointment, and with the company Porsche placed at his disposal, the diarist made his way post-haste to Nice, where he linked up with the Advertising Manager. The first headline on Sky News that evening was: 'Pepys gets Post as Ghost Writer'. A few days later there appeared in the London Times an open letter to the EU Commissioner for Human Rights, signed by Anne and Anna. It hurled such vitriol both at the bicycle company and the diarist that balanced international reactions, especially of the cycling community, could but tremble at the hellish fury of the scorned writers. They accused the company of bigotry, anti-Semitism, anti-feminism, callous disregard of animal rights, biased employment of men, scatological language (so she did hear what the CEO said), cultural myopia, linguistic discrimination and imbecilic worship of sport. They accused Pepys personally of voyeurism, arrogance, chauvinism and vanity.

But as things transpired, Mr. A. J. F. Goodbody-Chainey's vision for his company, and all the hubbub that it generated, was to prove, in the end, an airy-fairy fantasy. Matty and the hitch-hiking Franciscan had approached the Monaco border, tracked by the Advertising Manager in his Audi Quattro, Pepys in his Porsche, and the ubiquitous Sky News camera team. The front wheel of the tandem was only one foot away from the crossing line when the green lights suddenly changed to red and two little customs men popped out of their cabin as the transit-blocking barrier began to descend. Ockham saw it coming, grabbed Matty by the waist and shouted, 'Velociter, velociter!' But to no earthly avail. It was too late to hop off and the barrier came down like a guillotine just behind Matty, splitting the tandem in two. The monk was left sprawling in a state of shock at the four feet of the customs officials, in his hands a pair of denim jeans with a leg in them and, on the road beside him, three quarters of the battered bike, a rosary beads, a smouldering cigarette butt, the bull Sacra romana et universa ecclesia and two brown sandals all in flitters. Matty, captain now only of a terribly wobbly unicycle, sailed on unnoticed and unnoticing, while behind him at the border the douane men, in complete contravention of all Franco-Monacon trade agreements, were busy giving the anything-to-declare treatment to the Franciscan, the Advertising Manager, Pepys and the camera team. The customs men gave short shrift to the contingent of Englishmen: Ockham was accused

a) of being a member of a criminal organisation involved in cross-border smuggling of cigarettes – with the Advertising Manager (Audi) and Pepys (Porsche) the obvious ringleaders;

b) of breaking EU regulations prohibiting advertising/ sponsorship of tobacco products at cross-border sporting events;

c) of attempting to illegally export meat products without proper Department of Agriculture documentation;

d) of making a mockery of religion by using monachal habit as disguise (a crime considered particularly heinous in the Principality of Monaco); and

e) of trading in textiles without a valid business licence.

The cars and cameras were confiscated, Ockham's gallimaufry unceremoniously incinerated, the bull sacrificed on the burning pyre, and the whole band of perpetrators cast into eternal darkness in the deepest dungeons of Grimaldi's castle, there to chafe in adamantine chains until such time as a new wheel of fortune should chance to spin them a fresh fate in casino country, or a new order of events should re-define their origin and destiny.

Practised upon by industry, hyped up by the media, divested now of his denims and his dignity, Matty arrived in his red and green underpants and yellow shirt on the main street of Monte Carlo. But as the flame of the bull burned lower and lower behind him, the wheel of his cycle spun slower and slower beneath him, and with papal support now totally dissipated, he collapsed in the middle of the road, right in front of the Casino, utterly deflated. Alack, a perilous, pitiless place. An ear-splitting whining of engines, a nose-numbing stench of burning rubber, and around the corner at breakneck speed snarled the leading car. Coultard, British and leading, smacked his fire-snorting Red Bull straight into the prostrate vessel of clay and released an unexpected principle of double effect: Matty made sh… of the Red Bull car, but the Red Bull car cost Matty his two arms and the remnants of his tandem and he was sent flying through the air on invisible wings. In his element now, the man from Mayo was shortly after-wards picked up again by the gentle westerly breeze that had wafted him in off the Atlantic onto the shore at Mulranny. In transports of joy at the reunion, it now cradled him along high over the rolling Riviera hills and the azure blue of the Mediterranean, with loose clouds rushing to cushion his weary head and multi-coloured leaves matting beneath to form a mattress for his truncated torso.

High above the tourist beaches, the zephyr whispered in soft tones to Matty: 'Come with me, thou child of my aery bosom. Away, away and forget a while the strings and fardels with which those creatures of the nether world would fain have bound thee to their thoughts of clay. All my days have I been with thee, behind thee, beside thee. I never left thee. I have seen thy undoing, witnessed thy dissolution. They confused thee, cajoled thee, co-opted thee. They loved thee when they needed thee, weakened thee with wonder and would have worded thee with their base vocabularies. As I go on forever around this spinning orb, their samely wiles ever come wriggling up through the pores of this my superterranean world, and through those selfsame pores I sometimes have to rain down tears of sorrow to see those mortals so passionately dally. My no-time friend, I know what it is like when they press their pregnant fancies and are delivered of sickly monsters of the imagination. They tried it on me, too. One of their imaginers looked up when I was gently frolicking with a bundle of clouds o'er his head. Misconstruing our innocent elemental play, he called me the breath of Autumn's being, re-named me the Wild West Wind, said I was an alarm-clock wakening the blue Mediterranean from his summer dreams, an axe cleaving the Atlantic in two in order to terrorize the sea-blooms and the oozy woods on the bed of that great ocean. He called on me – like they called on thee, my dear, dear friend – to drive his dead thoughts over the universe and scatter his words among mankind. Just imagine! But I got my revenge, later, when he went for a swim in that selfsame Mediterranean.'

Suddenly Matty's bearer held his breath.

'Oh, I had not noticed,' he said. 'Time passes so quickly up here. Behold below, that's Genoa on the Ligurian coast. Thou art headed, I know, for the eternal city, but I must be true to myself: I cannot go south with thee, I would be encroaching on the territory of my sister wind from the north. I must leave thee here.'

Then that gentle breeze bundled together a few of the

more substantial clouds and, rolling foetal Matty up, now matured into an almost perfect mathematical circle, enwombed him in a fluffy sac of amniotic vapours, swaddled him with kisses and let him off, a messenger who had lost his message, down the coast towards Rome of the seven hills. The westerly breeze continued eastwards on its umpteenth trip around the world.

Pope John XXIII was feeling cross. It was three days now since he had got the tip-off from John XXII that missionary Matty was approaching, and still there was no sign of him. Proud, in a shy kind of way, that the long years of waiting for the hero's advent since his namesake's time were to come to an end during his pontificate, he left no stone unturned to make sure that the triumphal entry was a beer and skittles occasion. He had posted a welcoming committee on all main roads leading into Rome and had organized side-shows, peep-shows, pageants, brass bands, parades, fireworks, chariot races, jamborees, jazz gigs, bear-baitings, gladiator shows, jam sessions, masques, discos; for the children sack races, bouncing castles and pony rides in the Circus Maximus; for the more active fairground games, skittle alleys, casinos, quoits, dancing down by the Tiber and in front of the Spanish Steps. All transport, public and private, was brought to a halt, and at every street junction there were little stalls erected offering hot dogs, panini, sandwiches, barbecues, meat balls, panna cotta, pizze papali, with wine, wassail, mead, nectar, vino caldo, beer, lemonade, spremuta, mineral water. The traffic lights were re-deployed, the green lights now signifying that the stall beneath it still had sufficient reserves of edibles and beverages, the yellow lights warning that supplies were running low, and the red lights telling the hungry and thirsty to take their custom to the next junction. Banners fluttered from grotesque gargoyle heads, streamers stretched from cornice to pinnacle high above the streets and squares, and flags of every nation under the sun leaned dangerously out of windows. Throngs of dancers, distinguished and undistinguished, danced sambas, hornpipes, and boleros as the music from the loud-speakers boomed through the city, knocking more chips of mortar out of the old Colosseum. It was to be a red-letter occasion. RAI Uno was transmitting the great celebration live to every satellite-linked country in the world, and had hung up for the on-the-spot audience a giga screen that covered completely the face of St. Peter's Basilica. But where was Matty? Pope John XXIII was very cross.

But that morning he was cross for a second reason. It was frustrating enough that the stage he had so wonder-fully set for John XXII's emissary was still awaiting the entry of the main actor, but the vexations of the previous day had been enough to force him, in an excruciating battle with himself, to make the entry in his diary, 'John, do not take yourself so seriously.' It was all due to a computer mistake. Whether it was a virus, a hacker, a worm, a phisher or mere sabotage, he did not know, but the Great Ecumenical Council he had convoked was home-paged and e-mailed around the world as a Great EU Medical Council, open to everybody, and specialists and non-specialists who were in any way interested in medicine or health or sport sat side by side with the theologians and philosophers in the lecture halls, on the rostrums, around the workshop tables and at Council sessions. Total confusion had been the result. Aquinas, up from Naples, found himself faced with a sea of pro-foundly interested geriatrics when delivering his lecture on Potency and Act. Aristotle, on the other hand, found a more select audience of abdominal surgeons sitting attentively on the Spanish Steps as he walked up and down in front of them explaining his Posterior Analytics. Keats, looking down on the proceedings from his upstairs window and hoping that Flo Nightingale might be in attendance, sighed when he could not see her, closed the casement, and went back to ode her in his bed. Louis Pasteur and Joseph Lister took their autoclave and walked out of the podium discussion on The Ethics of Sterilization, chaired by Gabriel Fallopio over from Padua. They confided to reporters, avid for an interview, that they had been invited to the Council under false pretences and would most certainly be submitting a bill for travel and accommodation expenses to the Vatican. A Swiss Guard had to throw Elton John out of the Council hall for heckling Charles Darwin when delivering an address entitled 'From Homo Erectus to Homo Sapiens' to the synod of bishops. And a debate between Cicero and Edmund Burke on Oratory and Delivery was attended only by nuns, midwives and Freddy Mercury. At his wits' end, John withdrew to the Sistine Chapel for a brief respite from the concourse of people on the square and to pray to the Almighty for guidance. With a finger in each buzzing ear, he buried his face in his hands, not being in any way disposed at the moment to admire the very questionable creation of man frescoed by Da Vinci above his head. Had that creation been a good idea ultimately, he asked himself. A wise step? Scarcely had that seditious, rebellious thought disbanded itself when the deafening reverberations of a great commotion on the piazza forced their way around his fingertips onto his eardrums and, dreading another day of discord and disorder, he went outside again into the blinding light that radiated from the blue, cloudless sky. Cloudless, that is, but for one, lone, strange, foetal cloud that was descending slowly but directly over the pharaoh's phallic obelisk which stood in the middle of the square, representing the flow of life between heaven and earth. Some of the multitude were tempted to panic, but for some strange reason wouldn't; others were inclined to clap, but for some strange reason couldn't. Then a small girl, whose pregnant mammy had told her that God had created a little brother for her in heaven and would soon be sending him down to them, dug her elbow in her mum's still very rotund tummy and cried out, 'It's him, mum, it's him, it's him!' The cloud came lower and lower, the shape became clearer and clearer. The spark of the little girl's vision ignited a sudden flame of general recognition and soon the city was aglow with jubilation and rocking with odes to joy. When word spread that Matty was arriving by air, many misguided faithful on the city's periphery rushed south-west to Aeroporto Leonardo da Vinci to see him touch down. Others, hearing of an unusual flying object about to land on the city, feared a terrorist attack and fled to the catacombs. Above the babble and the hubbub on St. Peter's Square, the Pope's voice called out over the loud-speakers for the music, as arranged, to start. Little Mozart playing with the brass buttons on his gala coat and thinking of his next composition for wind and his next game of billiards, missed his cue. So his father lifted him up, brought him over to where the piano stood, plonked him firmly on the base of the obelisk and put a baton in his hand. 'The Skittle Alley Trio' he announced, and with-drew. But the pianist had gone off to the toilet, and the thirsty Corkonian clarinettist had invited the unwitting violist from Vienna to a bar to wet his whistle. So Nero, who was often seen hanging around the obelisk playing plaintive melodies on his fiddle to the monument that Pope Sixtus had stolen from his Circus, and for which he was still pining, was happy to step into the breach and help little Mozart out. Elton, bounced by the bishops, sat down at the piano to work his annoyance off. At a beck from Wolfgang Amadeus, the two musicians struck up, and they gave such a resounding rendition of the trio that Wolfgang would have obliterated the clarinet part altogether from the score had not his father intervened and rapped him on the knuckles with the baton. But nobody noticed the incident, and nobody was listening anyway. All eyes were on the nebulous appearance overhead.

Twenty-five metres above the earth Matty circled in his comfortable cloud, hovered over the cross at the top of the obelisk. The doors and windows of the lecture halls and workshops flew suddenly open as the delegates to the Council streamed out for their elevenses. Like everybody else, their gaze was soon fixed on the enigmatic cloud. 'Who is it?' 'What is it?' everybody was asking. Dissensions arose. Nuns and midwives and prolific campaigners raised their open arms and comforting voices, calling out to Matty not to fear to come down to earthy on their gentle bosoms, for he had no other choice. Some of the abdominal surgeons started handing out flyers that read, 'In the final analysis, away with it!' while others extended a long, telescopic, obstetrical ladder to deliver him safely to earth. From out the shadows of Bellini's columns there now emerged a dumpy little multi-child lady, with an osteoporosic limp, a ponytail, and short, pudgy legs. In one hand she held a small basket with two eggs in it, which she endeavoured to conceal and protect beneath a broad apron. She looked up at the cloud and would fain have made a bee-line for the phallobelisk, but the crowd was very dense. However, with strong, agricultural elbows and language, she battled her way through nuns, midwives, doctors, theologians, philosophers and plebs, pushing aside with particular violence the woman with the child. Shaking her fist at the cloud, she kept shouting in a raucous voice, 'Get rid of it! Get rid of it!' Then tackling the Egyptian menhir and the cross erected at the top (no compliment here to a monument), she struggled up onto the pedestal, pushed little Mozart off, and proceeded to mount the rigid, granite

182

monolith. Wrapping her short legs as best she could around its slippery sides, she slowly worked her way upwards. Then what started among the crowd as isolated calls of 'Three cheers!' 'Hurrah!,' 'Hosanna!' 'Up she flew and the cock flattened her!' gradually gestated into a cacophonous chorus of wolf-whistles, exultations, shouts, on-eggings, darings and bravado-gendering defiances. A Mexican wave started off somewhere, clockwise, and the sea of people on the square with the surgeons' flyers in their hands undulated around the doughty heroine, and she waved down to them in triumph as they circled beneath her. Applause, applause! Standing ovations! Then taking the two surreptitious eggs from beneath her apron, she flung them with terrific force against nebulous, vapourous Matty. The little girl looked up at the flying ova and thought they were little UFOs. Her eyes filled with terrified tears, and she began to bawl and boo-hoo and would not be comforted. In sympathy with her, other small children began to boo-hoo, too. Then the mammas and the papas, taking their cues from their babes, began to boo, and tut-tut, and cat-call, and hiss, and spit, and Gabriel Fallopio, with a symbolic candle in one hand, mounted the obstetrical ladder until he and the lady were on the same level, and shook his free fist at her over the heads of the people across the square. Then someone started off another Mexican wave, anticlockwise, and with candles in their hands another sea of people started a counter move-ment.

Great was the kerfuffle, then, that developed on the square, utter the confusion. No flurry of fallen leaves, driven to distraction by a skirt-lifting wind, could compare with it; no, nor no feathered rout of squawking hens flying hither and thither before a wanton, predatory fox. Where before had ever such a serried assemblage of hero-worshippers been so suddenly split into anti-types, antibodies, antipathies? Distraught, petrified, papa John XXIII got on his mobile to Paul VI.

'Have you nearly finished it?'

[- - -]

'Good. Well, sign it quickly and bring it out to the obelisk. I'll meet you there in five minutes. The situation is out of control, highly explosive. Human life is in danger! And, worst of all, the whole show is going out live on TV!'

He rang off.

Looking down at the seething, swaying masses from her coign of vantage, the little lady's head began suddenly to spin, an attack of vertigo came on, her strength gave out, and she slid with gathering speed down the burning flank of the monument. She landed heavily on the flat of her back beside the piano, feeling a sharp pain in her pride, and thanking the millions of lucky stars she was seeing that she was not dead. Freddy Mercury, who happened to be near-by, rushed to her aid with his thermometer, and then slender Miss Nightingale came along with her lamp and bent to aid Freddy. Roberto Gallo joined them, kneeling prayerfully on his Pasteur Institute document. Elton John, who had taken the distressed little girl on his knee when her tears came down and was soothing her with a gentle, motherly melody of his own, stood smartly up from the piano and, leaving the tender child sitting at the keyboard to keep his stool warm until such time as he should return, crossed through the milling crowds to the ladder and bounded up the rungs. Arrived behind Fallopio, he tried to blow out the candle the physician was holding. When that failed he endeavoured to wrest it from him by force. But Fallopio would not be dispossessed. A short tussle ensued, the ladder swayed on unsteady feet for a moment, and then toppled over. Gabriel hit the ground first and hard, Elton landed softly on top of him, and then they lay there motionless and benumbed, a source of hilarious diversion to some, of medical anxiety to others. The candle still burned in Fallopio's hand.

From behind the mega-screen covering the face of St. Peter's Basilica emerged His Holiness Pope Paul VI. In his hands he bore his *Humanae Vitae*. When he came to the monument, he solemnly handed the document over to His Holiness, Pope John XXIII, and the latter, appealing over the microphone for silence, commenced reading. Mr. Mercury, still bent over his fallen queen, looked up then. Without warning, towards the Pope he ran, snatched from his hands HV and from a Fallopio-follower a burning candle, and set the text ablaze. John and Paul tried to regain possession but Freddy held it aloft and started rock-trotting around the base, waving the flaming document in triumph. John and Paul texted John Paul II to come out and help them, and now the sainted trio trotted in chase after the flame carrier. The disunited mob started chanting support to express their varied allegiances. 'Hurrah, Freddy!' some cried, 'Keep going, Mercury!' 'Don't look back!' 'Fire away!' 'We get the message, Mercury!' 'You are the champ!' 'Up the Tasmanian!' Supporters of the popes litanized their encouragement: 'John XXIII, have no mercy on him.' 'John Paul II, have no mercy on him.' 'Paul VI, have no mercy on him.' Then, changing their tune: 'Up the Venetian!' 'Up the man from Milan!' 'Up the Pole!' Reviving with miraculous immediacy at the word, the little lady with the limp hobbled after Their Holinesses and pounded Paul VI with gnarled fists between the shoulder-blades. The second time around the obelisk, Gabriel Fallopio joined in the rondo behind the lady and gave a sharp, disapproving tug to her ponytail. If he did, he in turn was soon pursued by Luc Montaigner and Roberto Gallo who joined hands and, tapping Gabriel lightly on the shoulder with their *HIV* document, excused themselves and danced forward to partner the ponytail. Then Burke and Cicero joined in, followed by Keats who had finally found Florence. But his heart was aching because she had left again for her native Florence, where Alitalia had delivered her luggage instead of to Rome. The Olympic Committee joined hands with the nuns, each seeing in the flame a vision and a destiny. Cameras clicked, children cried, theologians with by-passes beat their breasts gently, microphoned journalists jostled for interviewing positions, delegates to the Council longed for lunch, and Louis Pasteur told a dirty joke to Lister. Aquinas and Aristotle shook their heads and went home.

In the blithest of spirits and tickled pink at the delightful hurly-burly, Wolfgang Amadeus, unchivalrous little Knight, snatched Nero's fiddle from him, hopped up onto the plinth again, resined the bow, and with a smile as broad as the locks of his wig would permit, made the strings of that instrument resound through the microphones with such sweet musical concord that waves of euphoria flooded into the hearts of all and sundry on the piazza. Spurred on by Mozart's golden strains, Nero, for whom Mercury was nothing but divine, and who was now all fire for Freddy's actions, if only for the reason that he had an axe to grind with the papacy since that obelisk affair, and who was possessed of a musical talent that transcended the ken of dull historians, took his place without further ado beside the child at the piano, and was only too happy to join Wolfgang for the gig. Mellifluous melody gave way to folk and blues and punk and jazz, rhythms rocked the pillars and towers and clocks, and peace and order and harmony descended with force upon the erstwhile swirls and eddies of the multitude in maelstrom. Now everybody began to rotate in the same direction, carried on an irresistible tide of benevolence and harmonious sodality, united in music. Mozart's daddy, Leopold, was the only one to glower and gnash his teeth as the wave carried him by his renegade son on the stage. The tired limbs and swollen eyes of the little girl finally succumbed to exhaustion and her drooping head came softly to rest on Nero's shoulder at the piano.

Mozart and Nero turned up the volume, stepped up the rhythm. The crowd circled faster. Soon those at the perimeter couldn't keep up with those at the centre. The rhythm got faster and faster. Then those on the inside, too, were pushed to the limit. Allegro, molto allegro, presto. M and N were now going hammer and tongs. Slowly, then, angularly, grindingly, raspingly, the obelisk itself began to rotate on its base. Slowly, but gathering speed, adagio, lento, accelerando. As the r.p.m.s increased, the obelisk twirled like a spinning top, whirred like a projector spool, swivelled like a whirligig. Mozart and Nero were sent flying off the plinth. Total silence fell on the crowd. Everyone stood stock still. They had all forgotten about Matty.

As they now looked up, the two UFO eggs came plummeting back down and landed unbroken back in the basket. Their unexpected return caught the domina off guard and she fell on the flat of her back a second time. In falling she knocked over Freddy behind her, and he knocked over Elton behind him, and Elton knocked over Keats, and Keats knocked over Cicero, and Cicero knocked over Fallopio and in no time a world record of knocked-over dominos and dominas were lying supine on the square under Rome's midday sun – an ideal position from which to view the scene that followed.

The monument was now spinning at top speed, like the turbos of a jumbo making ready for take-off. Then from out the cloud a little piercing shriek was heard above the whirr-hum of the menhir. A strange sound. A Munch's cry? A word? Nobody could say for certain. Then the amorphomattyembryonicloud elongated itself into a

187

tissuey cord and was sucked circling straight down through the middle of the phallirocketobelisk, ejaculating a harmless little fizzle as it disappeared. A barren thorn fell from nowhere onto the Piazza San Pietro. Then as all the bells in Rome boomed out the midday angelus, the tower lifted off slowly, leaned slightly to one side, followed a seemingly predetermined route eastwards, gathered speed, and was soon out of sight and earshot as it zoomed off into the round, fertile, infinite womb of futurity. RAI Uno ended its transmission.

*   *   *

Maria from Mulranny got up from her wedding-gift rocking-chair beside the warm turf fire and switched off the TV. A fascinating programme. She threw her Aran cardigan about her shoulders, for it was getting late, coming up to half past eleven, and they had forgotten to put the halter on the donkey for the night (or he might be off again on his travels) and close the barn door. Only the night before the fox had come and killed all of the neighbour's 25 chickens, and instead of defending the flock, the stupid sheepdog had gone and eaten all the eggs as well. The air was nippy now, though it had been a beautiful warm day, with a gentle, westerly breeze blowing in off the Atlantic. Down on the strand in a little sheltered cove behind a sand dune, she and Kevin had once more consummated their 2-week-old marriage. For hours they had then lain beside each other, looking up into the blue, blue sky, across which a stray cloud occasionally wandered. They re-lived the previous week's honeymoon in Paris, reminiscing about how they had first met within a stone's throw of the Eifel Tower when she was doing au pair to a wealthy, racehorse-owning, aeroplane-manufac-turing Parisian family, with two spoiled brats of children, and he was doing a three-month further-training course at the Paris Police Academy in Marne-la-Valée and, hating French, was pining each day for his home back in Kilalla and his own language.

'You know, Kevin, I married you for the wrong reason,' she said, pulling his leg again. 'In fact, for two wrong reasons! First, when I saw you parading down Avenue Hoche with the others I thought you were French, and I was so looking forward to a good flirt with a real Frenchman. And secondly, I loved your uniform. You see, with my father a sergeant, and his father before him, and his father, too, I didn't have much choice. You won me under false pretences!'

'And I fell in love with you just because you were blonde,' Kevin sallied weakly.

The afternoon had passed so quickly.

'I'll go,' said Kevin, bounding to the door first. He would no hear tell of her going into the dark. She might slip, or catch a cold or something, and that he would most certainly prevent.

'Not at all, I'll go,' said Maria.

So arm in arm they sauntered out together, tethered the donkey, closed the barn door, came back in to the warm and cosy kitchen, locked up for the night, and knelt down at the hearth to say the Rosary, knees on the hard floor, elbows on the chairs for support, Rosary beads in their hands

'What day is today?' asked Kevin.

'Thursday,' said Maria.

'The five Joyful Mysteries, then,' said Kevin, and blessing himself he started off on his rosary beads. 'The first Joyful Mystery, the Annunciation.'

It was Maria's turn to do the second and fourth mysteries. On both occasions she miscounted, saying the Glory be to the Father once after only nine Hail Marys, and the second time overshooting the mark with eleven. Somehow she couldn't concentrate, she was fidgety, she was uncontrated, her mind kept going back to the strand, to the cloudless sky, the lovely warm breeze rolling in off the ocean. She glanced sideways at her husband, deep in prayer. She glanced at the wedding rings on their fingers cordoning them off from the wearisome world of news and publicity and business. She gazed at the dying embers of the fire that were bringing a wonderful day to a close. A little spark ignited, burst off, and was gone. She smiled faintly. She knew. She knew for certain. There could be no mistake. It just had to be.

'Maria, of course, if it's a girl. But if it's a boy, what will we call him?' she said, to herself.